Title.

Slag shower

By Zeeshan Ali

Section 1:

Meeting

I turned my face towards the sky with a profound murmur, as I sat on the edge of the pack's domain partaking in the sensation of the downpour running over my face.

I cherished the downpour, adored the impression of the water washing ceaselessly every stressor as I recovered control of myself. I shut my eyes intellectually attracting the water to me feeling the quieting pattering of drops all over. Downpour resembled the universe's method of correcting all off-base.

Days like today there was a lot for the universe to make right.

'We haven't been neglected, we simply haven't discovered her yet.' My wolf, Brooke, whimpered toward the rear of my head.

'Sure.' I said unconvinced as I gradually made me fully aware of post over the sea observing how every immaterial drop hit the surface. I murmured, running my hand through my shaggy hair, brushing it out of my eyes.

'Richard.' Logan's voice blast through our psyche interface, making me jump.

'Indeed, Alpha?' I reacted deferentially.

I would have said something more snide to my dearest companion however I could feel different consciousnesses paying attention to our discussion. As Beta, I could never set an illustration of lack of regard with others around. At the point when it was only us there was no chain of importance. We were valid siblings in that sense.

'Have you completed watch yet?' His voice was trickling with customs and I absently contemplated whether he was preparing for a gathering or then again in the event that he had recently completed one.

Logan was downright awful at progressing from proficient discussion to relaxed; it generally took five to ten minutes for him to make the change.

'That's right.' I said nonchalantly. 'You need me back at the house?'

'No, really, there's a maverick close to town and I need you to confirm it's anything but a threat to the pack.' His voice was gradually losing it's strained tone, explaining that he had recently completed a gathering.

'Sure do you need me to drive them away?' I asked, feeling Brooke bristle with energy.

'That may be ideal, yet I'll surrender it to you.' His depletion was out of nowhere substantial.

'Everything OK Logan?' I asked, out of nowhere concerned.

'I'll converse with you about it when you get back. Trish is practically out of lemons could you get a few?' He said and I could imagine him ringing out his hands the manner in which he generally did to persuade himself.

I laughed recollecting that between being the alpha and his mate being eight months pregnant, Logan will undoubtedly be depleted.

'Obviously, let me know as to whether there's whatever else.' I said grinning to myself.

With that I took off running. In seconds I was in the timberland that lined the sea shore. I could feel every piece of turf against my exposed feet and I adored it.

'Shift!' Brooke whimpered.

I shook my head in one speedy jerk. It was my move.

Unexpectedly a chocolate earthy colored wolf flanked my right and a debris dim she-wolf to my left side.

'Zane, Rowan.' I recognized them.

Then, at that point, feigned exacerbation obviously Logan would send back up. I could simply hear him saying best to be as careful as possible for the millionth time.

The she-wolf, Rowan, gestured in light of my hello.

I saw a glimmer of red and orange and was unexpectedly worried that there may be a fire, yet I smelled no smoke.

'Shift Richard, there's two of them.' Rowan said her dim hide shining metallically.

I stop quickly to strip my shorts and store them with my shirt around my lower leg. Then, at that point, I let Brooke dominate. I shivered at the recognizable hotness that shot through my body as I moved. The others hadn't stood by however it didn't make any difference. I was greater, quicker, and more grounded than the two of them.

I surpassed them rapidly, hustling ahead and pursuing the fire that through Brookes eyes I could now see was a little she-wolf.

I could likewise see, Rowan wasn't right. There were three wolves.

The she-wolf utilized her nose to ask her young puppy forward, yet I could smell a male as well.

Abruptly the she-wolf's follower jumped out of the trees close to her clamping down on her right flank. Her tormented yell filled the woodland.

Brooke snarled irately, smashing the wolf in his ribs. He flew through the air smacking against a close by tree, the youthful maple snapping under the tension.

The male wolf was enormous with a sandy earthy colored coat and blood staining the hide around his gag.

He sprung to his feet snapping his extremely sharp teeth at my neck. I avoided the assault effectively and we paced gradually to and fro growling and snapping as we estimated each other up.

I was cautious with regards to keeping myself immovably among him and the she wolf who was falling down behind me.

I was greater than him yet he was quicker. He rushed chomping down hard on my front left leg.

I howled in torment as Zane, at long last getting up to speed, chomped down on the wolf's neck hurling him from me.

I constrained the raindrops closest to him to join and freeze strong prior to taking shots straightforwardly at him.

I brought down my head farther, growling at him as he pulled back attempting to move away from the pelting ice. Obviously with a straightforward push of my brain, the ice balls followed him. They pushed him farther and farther away from the young lady.

The disliking the abrupt change in the chances began stepping back leisurely prior to dismissing and running back towards the boundary.

'Zane, ensure he leaves the domain!' I snarled.

Zane gestured his enormous earthy colored head, prior to taking off after the outsider.

'You alright?' Rowan asked, poking me softly and positioning her head to one side.

'Fine.' I moaned prior to going to confront the she-wolf and her little guy.

I was unable to see the little guy behind where she stood defensively. Her searing red hide remained on end, making it hard to see where she was draining from. The growl she gave me was constrained and powerless. Her little body shuddered adding to the fantasy of blazes.

Unexpectedly her legs appeared to bomb her and she tumbled to the ground. I brought down my head in a token of harmony as I ventured forward with a delicate whine.

She growled pitifully accordingly, constraining herself back to her feet shuddering.

'She's harmed severely. What's with her hide? I have seen nothing like it?' Rowan asked cautiously.

'I don't have the foggiest idea.' I reacted battling the inclination to draw nearer, I didn't have a clue why I needed so gravely to help her.

'She's terrified of us. Mate is terrified of us.' Brooke whimpered.

I froze and gazed at her wide peered toward.

'Mate?' I asked him, looking as she avoided me once more.

Brooke just whimpered delicately accordingly.

'I'll be directly back, stay there.' I gestured at Rowan prior to support behind a tree and rapidly changing back and throwing on my remove jean shorts and white shirt.

Shock streaked through my mates eyes as I returned in my more fragile structure.

"Shift." I said smoothly.

She whimpered, battling my order. I wasn't Alpha however as the Beta in this region I had authority, and each wolf under me needed to regard that.

I immediately pulled my shirt off and threw it towards her understanding that she probably won't have any garments.

"Shift, presently." I directed once more, my profound voice repeating with a legitimate ringing tone.

I looked away as her hide began to wave and she moved. I paid attention to the texture as it slid over her body then, at that point, turned around. My breath was unexpectedly caught in my throat.

My shirt hung to her knees and as of now had splotches of blood smudging the white texture. Her long strawberry light hair was tangled with mud just as blood and hung in free waves down her back. Her warm earthy colored eyes gazed at me unnerved. Her nectar hued skin was a few shades lighter than my own almond complexion.

"What's your name?" I asked smoothly, concealing the inner battle against the frantic draw I felt towards her. She was certainly my mate.

"Myra." Her ringer voice tolled unobtrusively as she bowed marginally to my power.

I scowled inside, I'm not telling her. I don't need her to feel she needs to submit to me, for what reason would she bow.

"What's your business in the New Moon an area?" I asked mechanically.

"I..." She began, then, at that point, froze gazing at Zane as he strolled back up close to me.

'He's a distant memory.' Zane said serenely.

I gestured my thanks then, at that point, motioned for him to join Rowan somewhat behind me.

'What about you all go get lemons for Trish, seems as though I wont be getting to a store today.'

'You sure you're alright? Should we pursue them off too?' Zane asked inquisitively.

'Mine!' Brooke growled in head.

'At long last!' Rowan screeched enthusiastically as Zane jumped at my tone.

Rowan moved forward and Myra growled feebly. Accordingly Zane growled an admonition as Rowan froze.

'Go!' I snapped in kind, scowling at Zane, who as far as concerns him looked marginally abashed.

Rowan gestured then poked Zanes shoulder energetically prior to loping into the trees, Zane moved his enormous eyes following with a rough woofing laugh. Before he vanished totally he quit thinking back.

'I'm heartbroken, it was natural.' He thought, then, at that point, he was no more.

I, obviously, definitely knew this. Rowen was Zanes' mate obviously he would step in case she was undermined by any stretch of the imagination. That didn't anyway stop the displeasure I felt towards him for undermining my mate.

I turned around to Myra grinning plainly. "My expressions of remorse, proceed please."

"I didn't have the foggiest idea. We were, I was simply running..." She jumped as she said the word we, prior to looking behind me to where the other wolf had disappeared.

"Zane said he's a distant memory." I said refreshingly. A few seconds I included a doubting tone, "You didn't smell the fringe."

"Well yes." Her cheeks flushed red as she moved her weight gazing eagerly at the ground, "I trusted he wouldn't follow us here."

Unexpectedly the kid's face showed up briefly next to her.

He looked out with his dim green eyes wide, yet not with dread. He gazed at me in stunningness, his dark hair jabbing out at odd points. He seemed to be around five or six, which stunned me.

Since she was my mate she must be my age or less then a year more youthful. So Myra must be 21 or 22. She wasn't even mature enough to have a mate when she had a kid?

Regardless of the diverse hair shading h

Chapter 2

Broken

"Where are you headed." I asked, watching her intently.

I egotistically trusted she didn't have anyplace to go. Anyway as she peered down gnawing her lip plainly humiliated I felt my stomach stagger.

'Help her.' Brooke groaned wretchedly at me.

"Accompany me. You'll have a spot to rest and mend." I offered delicately.

"I don't think..." She began, shaking her head with her untrusting articulation fixing considerably more.

"Doesn't he need a rest?" I asked tranquilly signaling to her child. I didn't have the foggiest idea what I would do on the off chance that she said no.

'Chase after her till she passes out then convey her home. We can't forget about her here to kick the bucket, she's harmed.' Brooke snarled

'I know.' I reacted as I watched her nibble her lip thoroughly considering her alternatives.

"Mama for what reason is his hair blue?" The young man asked abruptly, checking out his mom to ogle at me once more.

I grinned as Myra's ears and cheeks became a striking shade of red once more.

"It's simply the light pal, my hair is excessively dark to the point that in some lighting it looks blue." I grinned at his own disheveled dark twists as he ventured out somewhat further. He didn't wear anything yet some fighter shorts.

"That is cool, mines do that as well?!" He asked strolling further away.

"A little better believe it." I addressed crouching so I was at his level. "You need to accompany me? I'm almost certain there's pizza and frozen yogurt at the house."

Energy moved quickly over his face before he folded his arms and frowned at me. "Is it accurate to say that you will hurt my mom since she's little, and you're greater than her?"

I looked into with perfect timing to see Myra in a real sense face palm with a profound moan.

Outrage erupted in my chest, yet I constrained myself to grin at the young man.

"No, I could never do that." I said genuinely.

"OK." He smiled broadly at me, "Frozen yogurt!"

This time I needed to laugh at Myra's exasperated articulation. She murmured moving her pale earthy colored eyes, before she grinned down at the kid.

She snatched his hand and began a few feet to one side.

"Are you OK to walk?" I inquired.

She gestured rapidly and I contemplated whether she might actually be feeling a similar attractive draw I was.

'She can't.' Brooke addressed my implicit inquiry. 'Wouldn't you be able to feel the dividers generally her? She will not feel anything until she believes us enough to let down her watchman.'

I could feel his trouble and agony on top of mine.

Fortunately we weren't left peacefully long enough for it to get off-kilter.

"What's your name? I'm Tyler however mother calls me Ty. It is safe to say that you are Alpha? Is that why I needed to do what you said?" The inquiries moved off the children tongue without space for taking in the middle.

I saw Myra solidify somewhat when he said Alpha.

"Richard, and no I'm simply Beta. Anyway in light of the fact that you are in my pack's domain I have some position." I shrugged inactively.

"So for what reason didn't you simply make Sye disappear as opposed to battling with him?" Tyler watched me wide peered toward.

"Tyler." Myra snapped, however she realized it was at that point past the point of no return.

Tyler had provided me a tremendous insight, they knew the wolf which implied he was probably hunting them.

"It's alright." I grinned claiming not to see the slip. "I was unable to cause him to do anything since he wasn't willing to pause and tune in. He had his psyche focused on a certain something and wasn't going to pause and think twice about. You and your mom were."

"Mother consistently says there are many courses all through some random circumstance. We must keep our eyes and ears open so we don't miss one." Tyler gestured gladly.

I grinned then investigated at Myra whose look was focused straight ahead. I considered what sort of circumstances she had expected to escape.

"Exceptionally shrewd exhortation." I returned my thoughtfulness regarding Tyler.

He hushed up for a couple of moments looking unexpectedly careful, practically apprehensive. I detested it.

"You OK child?" I asked, observing cautiously.

He gestured mindfully, and kept looking at me like I was the most intriguing and risky beast on the planet.

"Are you scared of me Tyler?" I asked smoothly.

Myra hardened. halting abruptly. She watched me one hand actually folded over Tylers.

I crouched before them, just a foot away, and met Tyler's eyes. Tyler looked anxiously at his mother prior to gesturing to me gradually.

"I'm grieved. I never needed to startle you. Your mother is harmed and I simply need you both to be protected." I talked delicately not looking away.

"Why?" I wasn't astounded when it was Myra who reacted.

"Since you're not kidding." I said looking up at her and acknowledging abruptly what an inept danger I had recently taken. "You don't need to trust me and I don't anticipate a single thing from you. I simply need to assist you with financially recovering."

She gazed at me stunned briefly prior to gesturing. I moaned as help washed over me.

"How could you become Beta? Who is the Alpha? Is he mean?" Tyler shot off one more round of inquiries as I stood and we began strolling once more.

Myra murmured yet remained silent this time.

"Logan is the Alpha, his father was the last Beta." I began.

Myra gave me a befuddled look prior to thinking down at her feet. It was clear she was listening all the more eagerly now.

"The past Alpha lost his mate, never remarried or had any youngsters. Anyway he embraced me. I was given the situation of Alpha yet I gave it to Logan and accepted Beta all things considered. No he's not mean by any stretch of the imagination. You'll like him." I grinned at Tyler.

"For what reason didn't you take Alpha?" Myra asked so discreetly that on the off chance that I hadn't had wolf hearing I wouldn't have heard it by any stretch of the imagination.

"Not what I needed." I shrugged looking forward. "I'm not quite the same as most wolves and I had enough to do simply figuring out how to control that."

She gestured as though this seemed well and good. It began to rain again and I began zeroing in my energy on repulsing the water from the three of us, I didn't need them becoming ill.

"All the force," Tyler said in wonder, "Father would kill for that."

Myra recoiled dropping his hand and abruptly wrapping her arms firmly around herself. It nearly seemed as though she was attempting to hold herself together.

Brooke snarled indignantly toward the rear of my head.

'Father?' The idea hit me unexpectedly.

'Duh, you think the storks dropped him off?' Brooke ridiculed.

'That is not what I implied, I simply need to know what it's identity is. Clearly he's a force monster.' I thought mockingly.

'That limits it down to two significant packs and around a hundred little ones.' Brooke moaned.

"A many individuals would, yet I trust poise is a higher priority than power. The greater part of those individuals don't contemplate that." I clarified for all to hear.

"But..." Tyler began.

"Ty no more." Myra's voice bankrupt as she wrapped her arms more tight around herself.

She looked sideways at me, her appearance while still marginally tormented was additionally befuddled.

I was thankful. While I needed her to know and trust me, I didn't know I needed to speak any longer with regards to my absence of interest in power with them.

In the event that she asked I would tell her, no mysteries or untruths. I got the inclination she would have all that could possibly be needed of those for the two of us, first and foremost at any rate. I trusted I would get every bit of relevant information ultimately.

"Goodness!" Tyler said bouncing around. "Mama, it's so beautiful!"

He was correct. We had recently entered a huge clearing encompassed by a rich dull green backwoods.

A three story light blue house with white trim remained in the middle encompassed by blossoms, all things considered. The rock drive was to one side and ran directly to the front entryway. It was fixed with flower brambles that were blossoming with many diverse hued blossoms.

I had thought it resembled a fantasy when I had been brought here at about his age. A while ago when I had accepted totally that I was reviled and had no future.

Right up 'til the present time I detested the word reviled, I had been persuaded that is all I was. Presently I realized it wasn't accurate and it was to me the most noticeably awful affront of all time.

As I suspected this I looked into feeling appreciative again that my father had been willing to take me in before he even realized how unique I truly was.

As the downpour ran down my face I could feel my body repulsing the water and I realized we would be totally dry as we entered the house. I realized it would bring up issues however I didn't need that white shirt to get splashed and stick to her uncovered skin.

Brooke murmured and I smiled as my heart dashed at the idea.

'I would cherish that.' Brooke snarled eagerly.

'You need everybody to see that?' I inquired.

His next snarl was angry, 'I'll kill any male who looks!'

'Precisely.' I laughed, acquiring a befuddled look from Myra.

She moved indeed attempting to obstruct Tyler from me.

I asked why she wanted. I hadn't undermined them in any capacity and he was only a child. Plainly not a danger.

I opened the entryway and grinned as I held it for her. She froze and I could hear her heart dashing. Following a subsequent she strolled in hauling Tyler behind her and absently sliding her hand along the entryway.

'Does she anticipate that I should pummel it on her or something?' I pondered.

Brooke whimpered accordingly.

"What took you such a long time Rich?" The dim virus voice repeated around the huge passageway corridor.

I naturally felt Myra's uneasiness increment and realized that this time basically she had a valid justification.

Myra's wolf snarled low and solid, a reasonable admonition as she battled to conceal Tyler from see.

Chapter 3

Dangers

In the following second I had put myself among them and the danger.

"Why are you here Azrael?" Brooke snarled as we stood protectively before Myra and Tyler.

'He's pulling them!' Brooke growled in my mind.

'I know!' I snapped back furiously.

"Mother." I heard Tyler moan.

"Ty!" Myra wheezed in shock and dread.

I stuck my hand out realizing that the youngster would not be able to oppose the sensation regardless of whether his mom appeared to be immaculate.

I set my hand solidly on his chest holding him marginally behind me. I could feel heat from Myra's dread on my back as I tenderly pushed Tyler back inside her span. In my fringe vision I watched her hunch down pulling him firmly to her.

"What do you have there." Azrael's voice was out of nowhere more bursting at the seams with interest as he smiled vindictively past me and at them.

No Myra, he could feel too as I could the force that repulsed his own.

He was a couple inches more limited than me with pale white skin and profound earthy colored hair and red eyes.

I growled the sound repeating off the dividers.

Azrael flickered gradually, moving just his eyes to me.

"So you at last discovered her. Really awful she's obviously harmed merchandise." He laughed, unmistakably entertained.

Myra's wolf, actually surfaced defensively, whimpered.

Brooke snarled angrily in my mind, and moved my weight obstructing them totally from see.

"What are you doing here?" I requested once more.

"Simply taking off. I had a gathering with Logan earlier today. I figured I would stay nearby to see my most loved maître de l'eau." His voice dribbled with bogus merriments. "Have you rethought my deal?"

I strained then with a similar convention expressed, "I'm not intrigued."

"However, no one here can comprehend you Richard." Azrael's voice was mitigating and I could feel him pulling more diligently battling not just for me now. "Not a solitary one of them could beat you."

I recoiled at the picture of battling any of my pack individuals.

"Fortunately they wont at any point need to." I shrugged, the movement jerky and sharp.

"You will adjust your perspective." Azrael snapped, vulnerability covering his voice. Then, at that point, he stepped past us and out the entryway.

Brooke snarled, as yet seething.

'Quiet down.' I said rigidly as I willed myself to do likewise.

'She isn't harmed merchandise!' Brooke growled at me.

'We both realize that.'

'Be that as it may, she doesn't!' He snapped, 'Didn't you hear her?'

'We can't do anything concerning that until she confides in us and accepts we are her mate. You going ballistic right presently helps nothing.' I brought up.

He whimpered yet I could feel myself quieting. I murmured profoundly, loosening up my head and shoulders.

'Consider the possibility that we frightened her considerably more?' I asked in a quieted murmur of an idea.

All I got accordingly was a sensation of profound concern.

Out of nowhere I felt a little finger jab the hand I actually had outstretched, palm confronting in reverse. I laughed then grinned down at Tyler who was watching me anxiously.

Gradually, abruptly depleted, I went to confront Myra once more. I grinned mindfully down at her. "I'm so heartbroken. I did not know he was coming over today."

She shrugged solidly, "dislike anything occurred. Much thanks to you for defending us." She said scouring her arm clumsily.

"Continuously." I felt my grin broaden.

She was so lovely; how could I get so fortunate.

"Would i be able to stroll with you now? When do we get frozen yogurt?" Tyler inquired.

I noticed him as he watched my hand, recoiling marginally, as I lifted it to pull my long hair back into a speedy bun.

Outrage and agony streaked through me as I understood he was hanging tight for a hostile move against him. Evidently he wasn't the only one by the same token.

"You can stroll with me Ty." Myra snapped tensely.

She moved forward close to him then, at that point, seen me gnawing her lips. Obviously she was not happy with how close that progression had gotten her to me.

I anyway was abruptly occupied by a stunning smell of downpour and pine. Some way or another they weren't exactly equivalent to outside however, it was better. Her smell was all that I loved with regards to rain and the sky is the limit from there.

"We would all be able to walk together. Kitchens along these lines." I grinned down at him after I paused to rest.

As we strolled through the entryway Myra breathed in strongly and froze. I realized she was feeling the tremendous measure of joined force from the other five wolves in the room.

They all halted and took a gander at her briefly prior to adverting their eyes. All with the exception of one.

"What the heck?" Rowan said, stepping over to me.

I felt Myra wince behind me however I just watched the modest blonde. Her wavy hair was pulled once more into a free braid. Her nectar shaded eyes were penetrating as she frowned at me.

She had no cosmetics on except for with her reasonable clear skin she didn't require any. Rowan was in single word adorable and had been similar to a younger sibling to me for quite a long time.

"You didn't give her legitimate garments prior to carrying her to meet the pack chiefs?" She proceeded with her frosty blue eyes piecing me.

I unexpectedly recollected that Myra was as yet in only my now blood smudged shirt. I felt a flush ascending into my cheeks.

I shrugged unexpectedly humiliated, "I... didn't.."

"Think? I know." She frowned feigning exacerbation prior to adding to Myra, "I'm so heartbroken, accompany me hon. I got something saved. We are about a similar size."

Myra looked at me and I grinned reassuringly, however I didn't know why she was unexpectedly following me. Not that I was whining.

"What's the story?" Logan inquired.

His dark fears were hurled in a free bun and with that his brown complexion and bruised eyes he generally seemed dull and baffling yet I knew better.

"I don't have the foggiest idea. She was being pursued. The child let slip that they realized the other wolf's name, so it wasn't some rush assault. He will fear you because of you being alpha that is actually all I got." I said gradually Logan scowled however gestured.

It was getting increasingly more typical that Alphas mishandled their force and however much he despised it he realized that the dread wasn't unwarranted.

"Furthermore, Rowan said the young lady is your mate?" He asked, grinning somewhat.

"Indeed she is." I grinned back splendidly.

"I'm happy."

"I bet ten bucks Rowan neglects to present herself." Jason said unexpectedly.

His splendid hazel eyes sparkled and he chuckled.

Layla, his mate, looked up to frown at him prior to tucking a strand of earthy colored hair behind her ear and turning around to her book.

I laughed, I didn't question briefly that Rowan would neglect.

"No," Zane protected her. "She's not so distracted."

Zanes nectar hued hair bobbed as he shook his head. His eyebrows wrinkled over his light earthy colored eyes.

"What's that darling?" Rowan asked, skirting once again into the room with Myra and Tyler directly behind her.

Myra wore a red tank top and some dark pants that embraced all of her bends impeccably. Tyler wore an immense men's T-shirt that I perceived as Zane's.

I glared, unexpectedly possessive and desirous that the little fellow wasn't in one of my shirts.

Brooke snarled possessively.

'What was that?' I inquired.

'I'm not sure...' He reacted timidly.

"Goodness hello angel." Zane said kissing Rowan softly on the cheek as she chuckled and flushed a dark red.

"I was making a bet that you never really acquainted yourself with the helpless young lady." Jason smiled, flipping his grovel shaded hair so it fanned across his temple.

Rowans mouth opened up framing an ideal O and her eyes were wide. She turned on her heel glancing back at Myra.

"I'm so grieved. My name is Rowan, this is my mate Zane we were the ones in the woodland with you prior." Rowan said hysterically.

Jason and Logan laughed uncontrollably as Zane pulled out his wallet murmuring something unintelligibly. I couldn't resist the opportunity to grin.

"I'm Tyler!" Tyler ventured forward, looking at everybody warily.

"Ideal to meet you Tyler. I'm Jason and this is my mate Layla." Jason, actually laughing, grinned at the young man.

"Hey!" Layla waved, putting down her book and waving. Her dazzling blue eyes sparkled with energy.

"Furthermore, I'm Logan." Logan stood strolling towards them.

I realized he was a similar stature I was, however close to her he resembled a monster. She was somewhere around a foot more limited than him thus dainty I was stressed for her.

"No doubt about it." Tyler said, staying away.

"That is the thing that they tell me." Logan grinned at him prior to going to Myra.

Myra jumped and bowed her head agreeably.

"What's your name?" Logan said, making a little stride back, doing whatever it takes not to unnerve her more.

"Myra, sir." Her voice was more grounded than I expected and when she turned upward there was an abnormal fire in her eyes once more.

"Ideal to meet you Myra. None of that sir stuff, on the off chance that you need anything let me know." Logan said, offering his hand.

Subsequent to jumping marginally she connected with take it.

"Poop." Logan jolted back the subsequent her fingers contacted his hand.

'Richard she consumed me. She is a maitre de fue.' Logan connected me.

'That clarifies a great deal.' I reacted prior to going to where she stood.

"I'm not terrible, but not great either sorry it was a mishap!" She cried venturing back against the divider.

She had Tyler behind her and her hands outstretched as though to give up.

"It's OK." Logan said, as I connected snatching one of Myra's shaking hands.

"No don't!" She yelled, critically.

She gazed down at our hands as dread then disarray crossed her face.

It consumed however I willed myself to ingest the hotness and cool her down.

Logan was certainly correct she could make and control fire. I could do likewise to water yet maitre de fue's are so uncommon. She was presumably the just one in existants this moment, while there's consistently four or five individuals like me alive at a time.

At last she met my look with a more loose and awed articulation.

Chapter 4

Not Alone

"You're alright, You are protected." I said crushing her hand daintily.

"How could you do that?" She murmured stunned.

"Tyler, hunny, you need some pizza and we can go turn on a film?" Rowan asked unexpectedly.

I felt Myra harden then said discreetly, "She realizes I need to converse with you. He'll be there in no time flat, you'll have the option to see him."

She loose leisurely then went to Tyler, "You can assuming you need to."

"Alright," He reacted reluctantly.

Then, at that point, he grinned at Rowan and strolled gradually over to her looking back. He froze most of the way there then turned around to scowl at me.

"Try not to hurt my mama." He snarled.

I heard a few group laugh, yet the outrage and agony in my chest prevented me from seeing any humor in his endeavor at a danger.

"Never." I reacted truly.

Following a moment of investigation he gestured one speedy jerky movement before he pivoted suddenly following Rowan into the front room.

Myra watched across the room and through the entrance while Tyler sat close to Rowan on the love seat and she gave him a plate loaded with pizza.

I contemplated whether she had even seen that every other person had scattered also.

"He's protected you know. You both are protected here." I said certainly.

"You continue to say that." She murmured, still not taking a gander at me.

"I'm hanging tight for you to trust it." I reacted grinning somewhat down at her.

"Try not to pause your breathing." She pulled her hand back and laughed pompously.

I pondered when I would quit feeling so irate at whoever had harmed her so seriously.

'Never!' Brooke growled.

"I'm heartbroken." She murmured, jumping somewhat away from my resentment.

"No, I'm not agitated with you. I am anyway going to chase down any individual who at any point hurt you.

She read me briefly prior to turning around to Tyler.

"I know how you can manage fire." I said serenely. I connected with brush my fingers down her arm, however she avoided my touch.

"I have never been truly adept at controlling it. I am so grieved, I can't really accept that I consumed the Alpha. I will get us killed." She talked discreetly. As she completed the process of talking she peered down at her hands with a dread, I perceived very well.

"I can assist you with controlling it. Logan would not hurt you. You are unreasonably significant."

"You chilled me off, you didn't get scorched." She met my quiet look with her own wildly confounded one.

"I can do what you do just with water, I'm known as a maitre de l'eau. You are a..." I began yet she intruded on thinking down.

I was seeing she was unable to maintain eye contact with me for in excess of a couple of moments.

"Maitre de feu, my mother used to consider me that." Her voice was low and calm, however by one way or another still crisp and clean.

"Indeed, so your mom knew what you were? Did she at any point show you anything?"

"No." Her sharp tone was such a course adjustment that I really began in shock.

"Alright," I clarified after I had recuperated. "Interestingly, you figure out how to control your capacities. They are connected straightforwardly to yours, and your wolfs, feelings. She should figure out how to control her feelings also."

"For what reason wouldn't i be able to consume you..." Fear moved quickly over her face and I looked as she gradually loose. I contemplated whether she was conversing with her wolf.

"What does your wolf say?" I asked Brookes interest overpowering me.

"She..." She turned upward confounded, "She doesn't think I need my safeguards against you. She's attempting to persuade me it's OK that I can't hurt you..."

I grinned generally at that, "Well then Brooke and I express gratitude toward her, however you could hurt me. Since I can balance your gift it takes a huge measure of will, or an exceptionally compelling feeling to hurt me. Anyway in the event that it helps you to have an improved outlook, you could."

"Brooke..." She mumbled grinning daintily.

Brooke seethed with fervor, even I needed to concede something about the manner in which her lips framed the word was elating.

"What is your wolf's name?" I asked in the wake of making a sound as if to speak.

"Coal." She said.

Unexpectedly she jumped somewhat.

"What's up." I asked, concerned.

"What do you need from me..." She gagged out, tears gradually filling her warm earthy colored eyes.

"I previously let you know Myra. I don't anticipate a single thing from you. I... We simply need to help." I said unfortunately as Brooke whimpered toward the rear of my head.

"I have nothing to give you." She demanded unobtrusively.

"All I need is for you to trust me when I say, we won't allow anybody to hurt you, or Tyler." I said smoothly.

"I can't do that now, perhaps not ever." She said moving ceaselessly marginally prior to meeting my look. "Regardless of whether you are my mate I will not allow anybody to hurt him at any point in the future."

"You both have that impression?" I requested to ward off the hurt.

She jumped observably, "We both need him safe, however interestingly we disagree on the best way to accomplish that..."

I gestured gradually. "Then, at that point, it's simply you I'll have to persuade."

I could see she didn't trust me yet I would substantiate myself to her in case it was the last thing I did.

"Would i be able to check out your wounds?" I asked after a long quiet.

"No I'm fine. I simply need some rest. They'll be passed by tomorrow." She shrugged.

"Then, at that point, let me take you to your room." I advertised.

"No, it's just five. Ty wont rest yet."

My initially thought was to recommend that she hit the hay while we watch Tyler, however recalling what she had recently said I changed strategies.

"Then, at that point, what about you set down on the lounge chair with him? You can rest and recuperate while he partakes in a film." I argued.

Looking now, I understood how depleted she truly was. How the skin under her eyes was a profound purple and her eyelids hung. I thought about how long they had been running and questioned she had dozed over a little while at an at once.

"OK." She moaned after just a moment of thoroughly considering it.

Subsequent to getting her settled I strolled a few doors down thumping generally on the last way to one side.

"How would i be able to help you Rich?" Logan asked as I pushed open the entryway.

I saw as he gazed toward me he flinched somewhat, so my disappointment more likely than not been self-evident.

"Cut the crap." I spat, "For what reason didn't you caution me?!" I hollered, surrendering in dissatisfaction.

He moaned and ran his hand over his face. "Quiet down alright I figured he would be gone before you got back."

"Well he wasn't." I let out an exasperated breath. "I strolled my mate straight into the line of fire. Imagine a scenario where he had chosen to assault."

Logan stunned me with a light laugh. "You would fill his lungs with water while she consumed him alive."

I couldn't resist the opportunity to smile at the thought as I ran my fingers through my hair.

"Tyler nearly strolled right to him." I shuddered hopelessly.

Logan glared, unmistakably destrubed by that idea. "So Azrael knows what she is? Is that what you implied by saying that clarifies significantly prior?"

"No doubt, and I could detect something was diverse with regards to her. Also when her wolf runs its hide looks precisely like blazes." I smiled somewhat, then, at that point, murmured. "He realizes she is something. He can't know what, however with the measure of force she was withstanding..." I shook my head.

"Do you figure she would go with him?" His eyes obscured marginally.

Brookes snarl got away from my lips at the trace of a danger. Logan caused a stir astounded and I took a quieting breath considering every option.

"Possibly," I needed to concede hesitantly. "In the event that he can persuade her and Ember that Tyler would be more secure there."

Logan gestured, quiet as could be, "Your mate bond will not stop her?"

"No," I groaned. "She's too monitored to even consider feeling it."

He gestured understandingly then took a full breath, "Alright then we need to ensure she realizes they are both protected here, and you need to break through to her before Azrael chooses to attempt."

I gestured gradually, "I have some help to ask from you."

He positioned an eyebrow smiling at me, "Since when do you inquire?"

I really wanted to smile back at him as I shrugged inactively. This is the way it should be with him. He truly was my sibling inside and out blood to the side.

He snickered then shook his head as he spoke, "Feel free to inquire."

"I need authorization to offer them impermanent enrollment." I said genuine once more.

"Why? Everybody here knows what her identity is. She will not require it here." He grimaced at me befuddled.

"She doesn't confide in us. She is extremely free and I question she'll be cheerful simply remaining here and having everything given to her." I reacted gradually.

"Well I could converse with her with regards to it later." Logan began then quit meeting my look. "However, she's anxious about me... Right."

He snarled discreetly then folded his arms over his chest.

"I'm grieved."

"No I get it I simply disdain the maltreatment of force and it is turning out to be so normal. Werewolves are turning out to be significantly more voracious and force hungry than people. We harm, surrender to the bloodlust and beat down anybody more modest than us. It irritates me, and seeing it first hand..." He recoiled falling once again into his seat with a moan, "It simply aggravates it."

"Hello we don't do anything like that, WE are not a piece of that so none of that we stuff." I murmured sinking into one of the seats opposite him.

"I know." He gazed at me, "How are you Richard?"

"I'm..." I grimaced uncertain. "I don't know man."

"You need to talk?" He asked reclining and folding his arms.

"I'm so glad she's genuine, and she's here but..." I murmured gazing upward. "I'm harmed that she can't confide in me, and I need to kill whoever..."

I moaned, incapable to really articulate the remainder of my sentiments. He gestured, "I'm sorry buddy, I can't envision."

"Likewise i'm not sure why she was running from that person when she could undoubtedly have beaten him." I added glancing back at him.

"Right, I never got the entire story." He said insightfully.

I continued to recount to him the entire story. From when Rowan and Zane met me in the forest till I strolled into the kitchen with Myra behind me.

"You ought not have run in front of them." He scowled at me. "However, i bet she was excessively gravely harmed and uncertain if she would win. In the event that she thought briefly she would lose and he would have gotten to Ty

ought After

I sighed relieved to find Myra asleep on the couch with
Tyler on the recliner to her right with a large bowl of ice
cream. I smiled then slid down onto the floor leaning back
against the couch by her feet.
"Why do you do that?" Tyler asked, frowning at me.
"Do what?" I looked up confused.
He hesitated. I watched as his frown deepened and he bit
his lips the same way I already knew Myra did when she
was nervous. Then quickly he shook his head.
"You can ask me anything buddy. I'm not going to get
upset." I responded calmly.
He didn't respond, only shifting uncomfortably in his seat.
I sighed, " Can I ask you something?"
He shrugged.
"Why are you so timid suddenly?" I asked, attempting to
sound as approachable as possible.
It worked his posture relaxed slightly but he still looked
afraid as he looked at his mother fast asleep on the couch.
"Mommy's asleep, she can't protect me now..." he
whispered fearfully.
"I'm not going to let anyone touch you Ty." I said
honestly.
"But you like my mommy." He said as if that fact
contradicted my promise.
"Yes?" I frowned, fighting to make sense of his logic.
"Grown up men who like mommy, don't like me." He
stated, watching me with a cautious gaze.
Brooke growled and I was glad we were on the same page
here.

"I like you, and I think we are going to be best friends." I smiled kindly at him.

I waited as he judged my expression before climbing off the chair and sitting down next to me on the floor.

"You're weird." He said nodding once.

I laughed in response. "Yeah I have heard that before."

"Can I ask you something?" He asked, looking again like the excited kid I had met in the woods.

"Anything." I smiled pleased that he at least seemed to believe me.

"Why are your eyes silver?" He asked.

I chuckled, "I don't know I guess it was from one of my parents."

"Which one?" He asked scooting closer.

"I don't know. My parents left when I first showed signs of being different."

"Wow, even your mommy?" His eyes grew even wider as I nodded.

"Did your dad leave?" I asked nonchalantly.

'This is low Rich. Don't talk to the kid about it, mate will get mad.' Brooke said irritated.

'I have to know if they're being hunted.' I growled.

'Just assume they are and don't make mate mad.'

I ignored him as I watched Tyler's face.

"No. We ran away after he hurt me. I don't remember I was a baby but mommy says the line won't go away." He frowned, then smiled. "You want to see?"

He pulled down the collar of his shirt to show a large silver bite mark on his left shoulder far too close to his neck.

Rage burned through me and Brooke snarled angrily. We both knew by experience how hard it was to scar a werewolf. Only silver, a blade coated in wolfsbane, or a bite from a wolf who has coated his teeth in poison would leave a scar.

To make it even worse, that meant the mark was not in the heat of the moment, it was planned methodically, and excruciatingly painful. I was only glad he was too young to remember.

'His own pup?!' Brooke howled furiously

"But mommy still always takes care of me. She says I'm okay now and it's just like her scars it doesn't hurt anymore." He said oblivious to my growing anger.

I took a deep breath and reached out sliding his shirt back in place. "I'm so sorry that happened to you, you don't deserve that."

His face was suddenly unsure he shrugged looking down at his hands, "I'm the reason she had to run from him. I'm the reason she's alone."

I couldn't help myself, as the first tears slid down his cheeks I wrapped my arms around him pulling him closer under my arm.

"That's not true and I'm sure your mom has told you that." I said seriously.

'If he did that to his son...' I started unable to finish the thought.

'What did he do to the random unmated female he got pregnant.' Brooke groaned miserably.

I trembled at the thought as Tyler buried his face in my side trying to hide the tears.

The next hour passed quietly and eventually Tyler fell asleep in my arms. I laid my head back feeling the sleep coming over me as well.

I had been patrolling all night and training new fighters the day before. I hadn't slept in over 32 hours and I was exhausted.

As I rolled my head I felt it touch one of Myra's legs and suddenly she sat up right. Her frantic eyes searched the room before landing on Tyler asleep on me.

"He's asleep." I explained calmly.

"Why," her voice broke and she cleared her throat. "Why is he laying on you?"
"He was upset." I shrugged, "I comforted him."
She didn't seem to know what to say to this but clearly was more calm and relaxed then before.
I had half expected her to snatch him up and bolt. Instead she laid her head down on the couch with a sigh.
"You have no idea how good it feels to sleep on an actual," she hesitated then shrugged. "Piece of furniture."
I nodded and after a minute she met my gaze and I realized, by the fiery red color of her eyes, I wasn't talking to Myra.
"I'm sorry she doesn't believe you... I'm sorry I don't believe you more. Please do something for me though." Ember sighed, looking desperately at me.
"Anything Em. We would do anything for you guys." I responded Brooke's excitement seeping through my voice.
She smiled tearfully, "Don't give up on her. She is stubborn as hell and beyond guarded..." she paused frowning now, "But she needs you if we are going to survive the next year. We have been running from our past for so long but I can feel it catching up to us."
"I won't let you die and I'm not one for giving up." I said, my voice was ringing with determination.
She nodded once then closed her eyes. I blinked and everything was suddenly back how it had been.
'Was that a dream?' I asked groggily.
'I don't know.' Brooke yawned.
However I was wide awake now as a howl broke through the silence.
Myra shot up again, her eyes landed on Tyler almost at once. This time however I was one step ahead of her. I stood handing Tyler to her.
"Stay here." I said urgently.
"I'll keep them company." Layla said as she suddenly

slittered to a stop beside me.

"Thank you." I said before I bolted out the door.

Catching up to the others I took my rightful place on Logans right.

'What's going on Seth?' Logan asked, allowing everyone to listen to the link he formed.

'Five unknown wolves approaching from the south.' Seth responded sounding nervous.

'Who's with you?' I asked desperately.

'No one is here yet.'

Brooke snarled as I allowed him to take over. I leapt into the air landing on all fours leaving shredded clothes behind me.

'Fall back Seth!' Logan ordered from behind me as I ran to meet him.

I was the fastest and best fighter thanks to my gift. I hated the idea of the sixteen year old kid alone against so many. I trained him, he was my responsibility.

Even with him coming back we met just as the other wolves entered the clearing Seth was in.

'What's your business in New Moon territory?' I asked authoritatively.

No others here ranked as high as I did. This was a scouting party, no more.

'We are following the trail of a rough who seems to have passed through here.' The leader of the small group responded calmly.

'What's it to you if a rough is in our territory.' I responded.

'She belongs to our Alpha.'

Brooke snarled ferociously snapping in their direction.

Just then Logan and the others caught up to us.

'The girl bears no scent of a pack membership.' Logan stepped ahead of me to my left, assuming his rightful place.

'If you won't hand her over at least be warned. She is

cursed, dangerous, she could burn this pack to the ground in a heartbeat. You don't want her here.' The leader growled.

'Then why do you want her?' I snapped.

'My Alpha has plans for her. He knows how to... contain her.'

I snarled at the implications behind his words. She was no more than a weapon to them, and somehow I doubted their methods of containment were humane. I was suddenly furious and I glared directly at the leader.

The gray wolf started hacking coughing as if desperate for air. Water splashed out of his mouth but my rage did not subside.

'Richard stop!' Logan linked only me, his wolf snapping at my front right leg.

I looked away and the wolf collapsed gasping in huge amounts of air. After a minute he stood and backed away, eying me wearily. All five of them turned darting back into the woods.

Chapter 6

Secrets

'What was that, Richard?!' Logan roared, turning on me, his eyes wide with anger.

Brooke just growled in response. 'She's mine!'

'And what do you think broadcasting your gifts would do.' He yelled through the link, everyone else was slowly backing away heads down. 'I'll tell you! It'll put another target on your back!'

'I'd rather it be on me then her.' I flinched.

Logan was my Alpha and even the Beta could only stand up against his anger for brief periods. In all honesty this was the first time I had ever had to at all.

'You think they'll forget about her now?' He snapped. 'You're smarter than that Rich.'

Brooke whimpered as my stomach brushed the ground under the weight of his rage. I shook my head I was still the rightful alpha and though I would not derespect him, I would not apologize for protecting my mate. I stood tall only allowing head to droop enough for him to know it was not a challenge.

'He said she's cursed Logan...' My voice was low and pained.

Logan flinched at Brooke's tortured whimper.

Logan sighed relaxing.

'I know. I know. I'm sorry I got so mad but I don't like you risking yourself this way bro.' Logan groaned.

'You would do it for Trish...' I nudged his neck with my head.

He glared at me for a moment before I added. 'I shouldn't have reacted that way I know. I just, I don't know he was

threatening her and saying she belonged to someone else and I just... I snapped. I'm sorry.'
He nodded. 'And yes I would defend Trish against anything in a heartbeat, no second thoughts or doubt. But I can't do what you can. You scare some people.'
I chuckled, the sound was strange coming out of Brookes mouth, it was a wilder harsher sound. 'Do I scare you?'
I had meant it as a joke but he paused deliberating, 'I worry that the fear others bear against you could bring unpleasantness down on our pack. However I believe that as long as you are willing to help, we can overcome anything.'
'I'll think it over. I may just hide out that day.' I rolled my eyes.
'This makes me wonder however, how many Alphas she has pissed off by refusing to be a weapon.' Logan frowned into the woods. 'I wonder if that's what she thinks I will want.'
'I don't know.' I shrugged. 'She'll tell me eventually.'
Logan nodded once then we headed back towards the house.
The whole way I thought about what he had said. I had never thought about how the collective fear of my power might affect the pack. It will be even worse when everyone finds out what Myra can do.
Once again I wished there was some way I could have hid what I was longer.
I stared at the ground as my feet slid through the still damp grass.
'You saved Logan's life, as well as those three other Alphas.' Brooke said confidently. 'They will all be on our side if it comes to anything.'
'That's four of the seven major packs. It's too even, people would get hurt.' I groaned.
The year before someone had attacked the northern packs

at a council meeting. I had no choice but to use my powers to protect the Alphas, and put out the fire the attackers had started on the eighth story of the hotel, just below us.

Now everyone knew what I could do, and at least two of the southern packs were vying for some sort of claim over my abilities. The third wasn't sure what to think.

Alpha Jackson was uncomfortable but his Beta, Clay, was an old friend. He was trying to convince his leader I was no threat.

The past year I had been laying low while Logan and Clay tried to make peace. I had thought it was going well but maybe I had been wrong.

'How bad is it?' I finally asked.

Logan sighed, 'Jackson is on our side but the other two are getting angry and insisting you become some sort of communal weapon.'

'What?' I snarled. 'You're kidding right?'

Brooke's furious growl echoed around the slowly darkening forest as we walked.

'Afraid not. Of course nobody else agrees even slightly. For some reason though Damon, Alpha of Blood Moon pack can't seem to see you and a person with rights. He is controlling the Shadow pack.' Logan frowned.

'Why didn't you tell me?' I snapped.

'I'm doing everything I can and it wouldn't help for you to stress it. You are in no danger right now.' Logan kept pace with me. 'I'm only telling you now because of Myra. If Azrael gets to her and joins the Blood Moon pack...' He shook his head, real fear crossed his face for the first time in years.

'She won't...' I comforted him, but I wasn't so sure.

'Your goal is to show her this is where she belongs and keep your head down.' Logan commanded. 'If you can't I'm afraid the pack will be destroyed.'

Late that night I thought a lot about what he had said and

with his words ringing in my ears I hesitated outside the door across the hall from mine. As I raised my fist for the third time, I fought with myself. I didn't want to do this, offer her a place in town farther away from me. I wanted her right here where I could protect them both.

However despite Brooke growling in my head, and my own possessiveness, I didn't want her to feel in anyway trapped. If I wanted her to really feel safe, I had to give her the option. Whether I liked it or not.

I sighed again running my hand through my hair. Finally I allowed my fist to rap lightly on the door. I silently hoped I wouldn't wake up Tyler, but if I didn't do this now I knew I would keep finding excuses.

"Yes." Myra asked as she pushed the door partially open.

"Can we talk for a minute?" I asked, smiling politely.

She pursed her lips and glanced over her shoulder. Then with a sigh she stepped out sliding the door shut behind her.

"How's he doing?" I asked wishing I had the right to ask to check on him.

"Tired but good." She said quietly then hesitated before adding, "Thank you, I don't think he has ever had such an enjoyable night." She frowned at my feet looking defeated.

"No need to thank me, we just want to help." I fought the urge to tuck a stray strand of wet strawberry blonde hair behind her ear.

She was so beautiful and I couldn't help but grin. Water rolled down her collarbone and I forced my eyes away from the white spaghetti strap tank top and black mini shorts she wore. Then something caught my eye. Blemishes in her perfect skin, scars. Knife wounds, bites marks, and even a bullet wound to her upper left arm. Brooke snarled menacingly and I fought to not return the sediment out loud. Heat bubbled up in my chest as the evidence of what horrible pain she had endured and the hands of evil men.

"What?" She stared at me nervously, and I realized I had been just staring for several long minutes.

"I'm sorry." I choked forcing my anger into the back of my mind. "I just wanted to let you know your options if you choose to stay."

'She has to stay!' Brooke argued.

'If we give her the option she'll choose correctly, if we take them away she will fight us." I retorted.

"Options?" She asked nervously massaging her own arm.

"Yes. There is a vacant apartment in town and a job opening as a waitress at a cafe. They are yours if you want, or you are more than welcome to stay at the house and either work or just relax for a while." I explained calmly.

She hesitated and I noticed something I hadn't before. There was a dark shadow on her white shirt under her left arm she was trying to hide from me.

"What's that? Are you still bleeding?" I asked, suddenly concerned.

She should have been mostly healed by now, only final scarring left. Certainly should not have any open wounds left.

"I'm fine. It's healing, just slowly." She said awkwardly as she tried to cover the dark patch.

There were two reasons something would be taking this long to heal. Either there was some form of poison in the wound, or her wolf was simply too weak to put the effort into it. This time I figured it was the latter.

I frowned, "Follow me."

She glanced back at the door behind her panic crossing her soft brown eyes. "I can't."

I nodded slowly, "Okay wait here."

I got back a minute later with cleaning spray, antibiotic cream, and bandages.

"What are you doing?" She frowned, not trusting me.

"Keeping it clean and covered will help your human body
heal it fast when your wolf isn't able to do it." I explained
Myra flinched and rolled her eyes.
"Sorry if I offended you Ember, I didn't mean to imply you
were incapable, just hurt and overly exhausted." I
chuckled.
Myra chuckled then sighed, staring past me.
"What did she say?" I asked Brooke's question willingly.
I couldn't wait for the day that I wouldn't have to ask. One
day I would be able to hear and feel everything, unless she
was purposefully blocking me.
"She likes when you say her name..." Myra blushed
frowning at the ground.
I couldn't help but smile widely as Brooke purred in the
back of my head. I had never heard him make that sound
before. There was a desperate longing to it as well as an
overwhelming happiness.
"Okay," Myra said after a second, "You can help me but I
would rather not lift my shirt out here..."
She glanced down the empty hall.
'No too many people could see her, she's not for their eyes.
Ever.' Brooke agreed eagerly.
"Okay we could step into my room for a second and then
we would have light and privacy." I offered calmly.
She shuddered at the word privacy, but didn't object
immediately. She stared at me for a long minute. Her
expression shifted as she conversed with Ember.
"Okay, but just for a second." She finally responded.
I smiled kindly and led her into my room. I turned on the
light before laying my hand on the door. I watched her
panic growing as I inched the door shut so I decided to
leave it open a crack.
"Sit." I requested gently.
She slid up onto the bed and watched my every move as I
inched closer to her.

"May I?" I asked gesturing to her side and she nodded
before flinching as she lifted her arm.
I reached out carefully rolling up the shirt that was damp
with blood.
Four thick lacerations stretched across her ribs just under
her bra.
I did my best not to reveal more skin or touch her anymore
then necessary as I sprayed the cleaning medication on
them. Gingerly I smoothed the antibiotic ointment over
them.
She flinched only twice though I knew it had to hurt a lot
worse then she was letting on.
"I'm sorry." I whispered as she flinched again.
"It's fine." She gasped softly.
I carefully spread the bandage across the area and tightly
secured it into place with medical tape.
"Here." I said stepping back and pulling a baggy gray t-
shirt out of my dresser.
I handed it to her then turned away waiting.
"Okay. Thank you." She said after a minute.
When I looked back at her she had the cutest most
confused expression I had ever seen.
I grinned at her before asking, "What?"
"Im just..." She hesitated, "Grateful, thank you."
"Of course." I smiled, thrilled at the turn of events.
She glanced at the door behind me then back at me. "I need
to check on Tyler."
"Of course." I opened the door then followed her into the
hallway. "Can you come back out and talk to me when you
are done?"
She hesitated then nodded slowly before walking into the
room.
I waited nervously for a couple minutes before she stepped
back out.
"I think I'll take the job and apartment." She said,

awkwardly rubbing her left arm with her right hand. Brooke growled, but I suppressed the frustration and smiled pleasantly at her. "Of course, I can help you pick up some stuff and set it up this week."

"You don't have to." She spoke softly and crossed her arms over her chest.

"I know, but I'm going too." I responded nonchalantly. "How old is Tyler, would you like to enroll him into the pack school?"

She looked shocked for a second before frowning thoughtfully.

I swallowed back a groan, we wanted so bad to know what she was thinking.

"I'll think about it. He's almost six." She finally replied thoughtfully.

Fear flashed across her face, her breathing quickened and I could hear her heart racing. Before I could ask though she spoke.

"Is the town... I mean the apartment... school..." she sighed frustrated before taking a deep breath. "Is it in New Moon territory?"

"Yes, you would be completely safe there, both of you." I didn't mention one of my men would be guarding them as often as possible.

"Okay." She sighed relieved before looking up at me with the cutest confused expression I had ever seen.

'She doesn't know why she is inclined to trust us.' Brooke chuckled.

'That doesn't mean that she really does trust us yet though.' I replied suppressing a grin.

'Ember does, you can see them arguing.' Brooke purred.

I frowned, not liking the fact I was causing friction between Myra and her wolf. I wondered if there was anything I could do to relieve the stress.

"What are your plans with Ty while you are at work?" I

asked curiously.

She frowned, biting her bottom lip.

"I hadn't thought of that. We haven't ever stayed in one place long enough for that to be an issue..." She confessed nervously.

"How did you guys get money if you haven't been working?" I frowned, trying to make sense of it.

"We mostly eat as wolves. I have taken a shirt and or underwear from clothes lines, but we mainly just stay wolves. It's actually weird to be on two feet again." She blushed ducking her chin.

"I'm so sorry you guys have been going through that." I sighed sadly. "You won't have to again. I'm sure one of the girls would watch him whenever you need, and I can help whenever I'm not working."

"Maybe." She said after a minute.

"Will you let me take you to lunch tomorrow?" I asked suddenly, surprising us both.

"No." She shook her head taking a small step back towards her door.

'Ouch.' Brooke said half heartedly.

I forced a chuckle, "That fine. Rowan wanted to take you shopping anyway, both of you. I'll have Zane help me work on moving you into the apartment."

"I don't have anything to move." She crossed her arms and frowned suspiciously at me.

I laughed under my breath then winked at her saying, "Don't worry, you will."

Before she could argue I turned and walked back into my room.

Chapter 7

New Home

The next day Zane and I left early to go furniture shopping. Before we left I asked Layla and Rowan to take Myra and Tyler shopping. They agreed ecstatically.
Zane and I spent the day carrying and setting up beds, dressers, a couch, and any other furniture.
"Ouch! Damn it I hate electricity." I snapped, fighting to hook up the TV and DVR.
Zane laughed out loud as he walked in from the back bedroom. "Can't say I'm surprised, water and electricity never mix well. Let me do that, you finish setting up Ty's bed."
"Thanks." I grumbled.
I had always known of the down sides to my power, but electricity had always been my kryptonite. I conducted electricity on a scale far larger than your average human. I walked back into the back bedroom and was able to set up the bed and dresser before my phone dinged.
Rowan had texted me; "On our way. What apt number?"
I responded with a thank you and told her we would meet them downstairs, then headed out to the main room with Zane.
"They will be here in a couple minutes." I couldn't help the excited smile that spread across my face. "We should go help them carry stuff in."
"Sure." He chuckled in response.
We headed out the door and past the pool towards the parking lot.
"So remember the apartment was pre furnished, she's going to be mad enough about the clothes and food and

other stuff." I rubbed the back of my neck sheepishly.
By now we stood at the edge of the lot

"She'll appreciate it later, you're doing the right thing."
Zane clapped my shoulder as Rowan's blue BMW X6
pulled up in front of us.

As the door opened a beautiful little blonde girl with
ringlets and light brown eyes jumped out and ran towards
us.

"Daddy daddy! I missed you!" Avrily yelled, running into
Zane's open arms.

"Hey princess. How was your sleepover at Jessica's?"
Zane smiled, placing the four year old on his hip.

"Perfect!" Avrily beamed.

"Were you good?" Zane asked.

Rowan came over chuckling and kissed his cheek.

"According to Jess's mom they were little angels."

"Well like mother, like daughter." Zane grinned down at
Rowan, his eyes shining.

I couldn't help but smile. Zane and Rowan had been lucky
with finding their mates. They had been best friends since
elementary school and dated throughout high school.
Nobody was really surprised when on Rowan's eighteenth
birthday they verified that they were in fact mates. They
had Avrily just over a year later.

"Can someone please help us?" Layla's asked awkwardly.

Now, as I turned towards the car, the pang of jealousy I
always felt vanished.

Myra was talking quietly to Layla while handing lighter
bags to a very excited Tyler. Tyler bounced up and down
and Myra was smiling. I had never seen her really smile
before and the sight took my breath away.

"Hi Mr. Richard!" Tyler said as he walked up, grinning
widely. "Thank you for my new clothes!"

"Of course Ty, and call me Rich bud." I smiled at him.
I reached down to ruffle his hair. He flinched away

slightly before blushing bashfully.

"Sorry." He hung his head embarrassed.

"Don't be buddy, it's not your fault." Brooke snarled in the back of my head and I forced a smile. "Let me grab some bags then I'll lead you to your new room, okay?"

"Okay." He smiled back at me.

Something in me shifted and I knew, even if Myra never wanted to be with me, I would always want to be there for Tyler. I had heard only a few cases where one mate had a child before finding the other. Knowing you have someone out there waiting for you makes most people hold off on intimacy. The stories I had heard mentioned a theory that the mate bond would spread. That by being part your mate you are automatically drawn to the child as well.

I had never put much stock in these tales until this moment when I realized, I loved Tyler.

It took several trips to haul everything inside. When we were finally done I sent Zane home with the others and insisted on staying to help put everything away.

First I helped Ty start a load of his new clothes before heading into the kitchen to start on groceries. Myra was already there dividing meat meticulously into meal sized portions to freeze.

She glanced up cautiously as I grabbed a gallon of milk and bag with refrigerator food in it. I carried it to the fridge and started putting everything in.

"You don't need to do that." Myra's voice was quiet but still sounded annoyed.

I grinned ignoring her statement. "Did you have a good day?"

"Yes." She admitted tentatively. "I'm paying you back though."

"Good, do I get a say in how?" I asked, turning to face her.

She eyed me nervously and swallowed hard. Her eyes suddenly burned with the same fire from when she burned Logan, fear. I could hear her heart speed up and realized my mistake.

"I mean I would love it if you would allow me to take you out." I added quickly.

She frowned surprised before taking a deep breath.

"How is allowing you to spend more money on me, paying you back?" She crossed her arms.

"I have more money then I know what to do with, if you give me more it'll sit in the bank completely useless." I grinned, taking a small step towards her. "However every second I get to spend with you is worth more than all my money."

I had been planning that since the night before, and the blush that spread across her cheeks was definitely worth it.

I reached out slowly and gently brushing a stray strand of hair off her cheek. She flinched but only slightly before subconsciously relaxing into my touch.

"Please?" I added quietly.

"I don't..." She started before biting her bottom lip.

My heart dropped if she said no now, I wouldn't give up but it would hurt.

"Can I think about it?" She finally asked quietly.

I sighed relieved then nodded. "Of course, just let me know."

"How?" She asked, stepping back and turning back to the grocery bags.

I chuckled lightly, pleased at how flustered she suddenly seemed.

"The apartment has a landline, I left a paper with some phone numbers in case you need anything. Mines there." I didn't mention that I was going to have somebody watching the building at all times as long as she was here.

"Oh, it's amazing that it came pre furnished with no down payment." She glared at me knowingly.

I shrugged, stifling a laugh. She wasn't going to get me to admit anything that easily.

"You're just lucky I guess." I winked at her.

I watched as her expression suddenly turned pained than guarded.

"No I'm not." She said looking back at the meat on the counter.

I sighed sadly before grabbing more groceries.

That night I stayed up late getting caught up on my work. The past two days I had been focused on Myra and Tyler, and that was okay. However, I knew if I was so lucky as to keep them in my life, I needed to learn to make time for them and work.

Especially if what Logan had said was true, I had to do everything I could to protect my friends and family. I owed them everything, and knowing that I would possibly be the reason for their downfall killed me.

'You can't think like that Rich.' Brooke sighed, 'You know we would do anything to protect this pack.'

'Yeah but if Azrael gets to Myra, I don't think I could ever hurt her.' I moaned.

'Well you don't have to worry about that because he will never get close enough to try.' Brooke snarled.

"I'm surprised you're home." Trisha's voice sounded from the doorway.

I turned slowly to see her standing just inside the door. Trishana was a couple inches taller than her twin Layla otherwise they were identical. With the same light rose toned skin and straight brown hair. Those deep blue eyes that seemed to engulf anything they touched.

"Luna," I nodded at her respectfully and she rolled her eyes.

"None of that right now please. I'm as big as a whale and

exhausted. My patience is nonexistent." She groaned walking into my room and sitting on the edge of the bed. I swiveled in my chair away from my desk to face her.
"To what do I owe the pleasure?" I chuckled.
"I just wanted to tell you in person I am happy for you. I can't wait to meet your mate, and her son. You got the package deal." She eyed me nervously.
"I really did." I grinned, "She is perfect, and Tyler." I laugh out loud. "He is so smart and curious about everything."
"So you aren't mad she already has a pup?" Trisha asked finally getting to the point.
"No, I mean I was a little shocked at first. Especially with how old he is, but I already love the kid. He is just as much mine as she is." I said confidently.
"What about his biological dad?" Trish asked, leaning back on the bed and studying me.
"All I know is Myra took Ty and ran after his father coated his teeth and bit his shoulder. The scar is so close to his neck I wonder if it was an attempt to kill the child and maybe Myra got to him barely in time or something." I frowned at the floor as Trish shuddered.
"God, that is horrible." She gasped wrapping her arms protectively around her swollen abdomen.
I nodded grimly.
"Well at least they have you now. As well as a whole pack willing to do anything for you." Trish smiled before standing with a groan. "We love you Rich, and I really am happy for you."
"Thanks Trish." I smiled half-heartedly.
I felt as though I had just been slapped in the face.
Yes a whole pack willing to do anything for me, while I was quite possibly bringing a bloodbath down on them. No, I would fix this. I had to fix this.
'With Myra on our side there would be no contest.'

Brooke mused

'I will not see her as a weapon, and I don't want her anywhere near a fight.' I snapped in return.

'You're right. You know I didn't mean it as her being a weapon, just our partner.' Brooke whimpered.

I sighed, I knew he was right. I would never try to use Myra to fight for me, but I would be willing to train her to fight with me if she wanted to.

However before I could even think of that she had to trust me. It was unbelievable how hopeless I suddenly felt, as if I had already lost the war.

Next to me my phone pinged, Myra's landline flashing across my screen. I picked it up quickly terrified something was wrong.

"Hello?" My voice was too cloaked to portray the nonchalance I wanted.

"Ok..." Myra's voice was low and unsure.

I was confused, what was she trying to say, but before I could ask she sighed then continued.

"But only if Rowan can watch Tyler, otherwise no deal." Her voice was stronger than before but still shaken, afraid.

It hurt that she was so clearly afraid of me. I had to prove myself to her, and now I had a chance to start.

"Great, I'll talk to Rowan. Do you work tomorrow night?" I asked, unable to stop the smile spreading across my face from coating my voice.

"No I don't." She sounded like she might be smiling too, or maybe that was just wishful thinking.

"I'll pick you guys up at four." I was already making plans.

"Ok." She said before hanging up leaving the dial tone ringing in my ear.

"Ok." I repeated, hanging up the phone.

'Well it's something.' Brooke sighed.

'No.' I grinned widely, 'It's everything.'
Brooke rolled his eyes, 'Since when are you such a romantic?'
'I'm not sure.' I admitted.
'I am.' He chuckled.
I rolled my eyes, turning back to my computer and began planning. I would make this the best decision she ever made.

Chapter 8

Family

The next day I kept track of Myra's actions though Jacobs mind link while I made preparations for the best date she had ever had. Which if I was being honest, the bar was probably set pretty low.

However if I was going to change her mind about me, this had to be perfect.

At 3:45 I was parked outside her apartment building. I was wearing my nicest dark wash jeans and a white button up T-shirt with my favorite black leather jacket as well as my favorite black combat boots.

I nervously climbed out of the car and headed up the stairs. Her apartment was on the second story of the complex. After a deep breath I knocked quietly on the door.

"One second!" I heard Myra call through the door.

"I'll get it mommy," Tyler said, opening the door.

"No!" Myra called, but it was too late.

"Hey Tyler how are you doing today?" I asked.

"Good. I got cereal and milk for breakfast!" Tyler stayed jumping up and down.

It struck me once again how things most children took for granted, Tyler thrived on. He had already had so little in life that even the little things were monumental to him.

"That sounds so good!" I exclaimed.

I was unsure as to whether I should come in. On one hand the door was open on the other Myra had told Ty not to open it. Before I could get too awkward about it, Myra appeared in the hall across the living room.

"Ty you don't just open the door when someone knocks."

She said smiling shyly at me.

All my nervousness vanished at the sight of her. Her hair had been curled and now hung loosely down her back. She wore only a small amount of eyeliner and mascara that made her warm brown eyes pop.

She wore a red v-neck blouse that hung loosely over her torso, making my imagination run rampant, and a pair of dark blue jeans and wedge heels. She looked absolutely stunning.

"Wow." I managed with a grin, "You look amazing."

"You don't look bad yourself." She said after a brief hesitation.

"Thank you. Now we should get going Rowan and Avrily are looking forward to spending the afternoon with you mister." I grinned down at the little boy and offered him my hand.

He flinched slightly, but quickly recovered and grabbed on my hand as if it were a lifeline.

I had to fight to not gawk at Myra. She was everything I had ever dreamed of and more. However I knew my staring would make her uncomfortable. I couldn't help glancing at her as we walked to the car and climbed in.

"What?" She asked self consciously.

"Sorry, you just look perfect." I said weakly.

She blushed and shifted awkwardly in her seat.

"Anyway, let's get going. Ty are you buckled up?" I asked to ease the tension.

"Uh-huh. Ms Rowan showed me how when we went shopping!" He responded excitedly.

"Good." I grinned back at him in the mirror.

'Well at least one of them likes us.' Brooke grumbled.

I simply rolled my eyes in response, he knew better.

It took longer than I expected to drop Tyler off. Even when Rowan had finally convinced Myra that she had it all under control, it was clear Myra was still nervous.

"When was the last time you left him with someone else?"
I asked curiously.
"Never."
"You never once left him with anyone, not even his
father?" I said stunned before remembering the little I did
know of Tyler's father. Of course she hadn't left Ty with
that abusive psychopath.
She shook her head calmly, unfazed.
"Sorry, I didn't think." I apologized suppressing my anger.
She just shrugged before asking, "Where are we going?"
"It's a surprise." I grinned halfheartedly, still trying to
shake off both Brooke's rage and my own.
"I don't think I like surprises." She admitted cautiously.
"Then you haven't ever had the right kind of surprise."
She shot me a disbelieving look. "Do you trust me?"
"No." She said automatically.
'Ouch...' Brooke groaned and I winced.
"I mean, not quite yet. I'm trying. I'm sorry that's the best
I can do right now." She flushed cherry red as she said
this. "I just don't really trust anyone anymore."
"I know, but I won't let anything happen to you. You are
safe with me." I pushed, determined to make her believe
it.
She nodded then frowned thoughtfully.
"Can I ask you a question?" She asked cautiously.
"You just did." I chuckled, "Lucky for you, you are
allowed to ask as many as you want."
"What did you talk to Tyler about that first afternoon?"
She asked, frowning slightly.
"What do you mean?" I stammered.
'Busted, I warned you!' Brooke growled.
"I don't know he just isn't known to fall asleep on random
guys shoulders. He's more cautious than that. He trusts
you." She explained slowly.
"Well we talked about parents mostly. Mine," I looked at

her guiltily, "And his."

Myra stiffened slightly but she didn't scream at me. I wondered if that was because of the fear or if she just wasn't one to scream and yell.

"You asked my five year old about my ex?" She clarified.

"No. I mean yes, not exactly."

She faced me glaring furiously.

"I asked if his dad had left." I admitted wincing at the daggers she was shooting me.

All traces of her previous fear gone, she looked down right dangerous. It seems ludicrous to me that some body so small could ever look so threatening. However it suddenly made sense that Tyler felt safer with her around. The car felt suddenly warmer than it should be and I rolled down the windows.

"Please don't set my car on fire, I know I crossed a line." I said quickly, "I'm sorry."

She rolled her eyes, "I would appreciate it if you would refrain from bringing Victor up around Ty. It's a touchy topic."

I nodded, "Of course. I really am sorry, I was just curious. Brooke was pissed at me."

She chuckled, the melodic sound surprising me. "Sorry." She murmured, "What did he tell you?"

"He said you guys left when he hurt Ty." My knuckles turned white as my fingers tightened around the steering wheel. "I can't imagine why he did that."

Myra shrugged.

"Let's talk about something more pleasant." I sighed.

"How about we get to know each other a little bit?" I suggested.

She sighed, "I guess that could be okay."

"Do you have any family?" I was unsure what exactly I was allowed to ask, but that seemed safe.

"Yeah, um. I have my dad and twin brother." She

responded.

"Are you close with them?" I was trying to understand why she was here on her own if she had family somewhere out there.

"I was really close to my brother, um I try to write to him whenever I get a chance. I haven't gotten to talk to him much lately. I don't want to drag him down with me." She smiled but I could hear the sadness in her voice.

"And your dad?"

"No, not really." She shrugged again, "Don't get me wrong he raised Trystan and I. I will always be grateful we were able to stay together, but he drank excessively and tended to be a little heavy handed."

"He hit you?"

"Honestly Trystan normally stepped in. He took the majority of the knocks." She corrected.

I nodded numbly.

"So much for something more pleasant, I'm sorry." She said again.

"I asked and I would love to meet your brother. He sounds awesome." I smiled over at her.

To my surprise she smiled widely, "Yeah, he is. He's an idiot sometimes, but loyal and always willing to do anything for me. He is constantly asking where I am because he wants to come see us. He really wants to meet Ty."

"He hasn't met Tyler?" I asked, shocked.

"Nope," Her smile faltered for just a second, "Tyler is so much like Trystan was at his age though. All the questions, that's Trystan through and through. Alway talking and normally joking. I have found very few things he is serious about."

I was enjoying listening to her talk. She hadn't spoken so much in total in front of me. The way she smiled and her eyes lit up it was clear that she had a strong connection with her brother.

"Well you should invite him to visit. Since your flight finally landed." I suggested.

"I might..." Her smile faded. "I don't know how long we are staying though Richard. I don't want to endanger anyone here, and eventually people will follow me here." I didn't point out that they already had. I also didn't want to argue with her. Luckily I didn't have to respond because just then we arrived at our destination.

"Here we are." I pulled over onto the side of the road. I watched as she looked around a hint of her previous fear reappearing on her face.

"There's nothing here." She said hesitantly.

"Trust me," I said not asking this time.

"Probationary," She agreed slowly making me smile.

"Well that's better than I expected." I laughed and she shot me an incredulous look. "Come on. I won't let anything happen to you, I promise."

For a long moment she hesitated in the car. Finally though she sighed and climbed slowly out of the passenger door.

Chapter 9

Date

As I led her through the woods I was glad to see that she seemed comfortable.

"Can I ask you a question?" I asked suddenly.

"Sure." She responded in a whisper.

She smiled slightly as we walked. I caught myself staring at the way the sun shone through the trees and glistened off her strawberry blonde hair. The red tones in her hair intensified natural pink in her cheeks. She was stunning and I couldn't remember what I was going to ask.

After a minute she glanced at me and frowned, "What is it."

'Smooth..." Brooke commented smugly.

'Why didn't you snap me out of it?' I snapped.

Brooke was silent.

'You were staring too.' I clarified, annoyed.

"You seem pretty comfortable alone here with me, why is that?" I smirked, cocking my eyebrow at her.

'Nice save.' Brooke smirked.

To my surprise she chuckled.

"You are in my turf now." She shrugged. "I feel more comfortable in the woods."

"We were in the woods that first day." I pointed out.

She flinched slightly. "Yeah, I wasn't doing really well. I was hurt and I was worried you or somebody else would hurt Tyler."

I nodded and slid my hands into my pockets, I had known that. I still didn't like thinking about it. I couldn't help but long for the day that she trusted me. Not only with her own safety but her sons as well.

"What did you mean by this is your turf though?" I grinned arrogantly at her. "These are my woods."
She smiled, "The last three years Ty and I have lived out in the woods. Honestly the last forty eight hours in doors have seemed almost suffocating."
Shrugged awkwardly. For the first time since we started walking her smile faded away. She tugged at her sleeves awkwardly and let her head drop so she was watching her feet.
"What's wrong?" I asked, unable to stop myself as I watched the pain flash in her brown eyes.
She took a deep breath and forced a smile. "Nothing, just thinking."
She shrugged passively before straightening again. Her posture was no longer relaxed though and her expression was tight and pained.
"Please?" I asked relenting to not ask again if she didn't answer.
She just shrugged and after another minute of walking we were there. There was a rusty old trampoline in the middle of a tiny clearing of trees.
"Wow, that's random." She said, staring at the trampoline.
I laughed "I know right. The guys and I found it in high school and it sort of became our get away when we needed a break from training."
"Huh," she replied thoughtfully.
"Anyway, I brought food and drinks. I figured we could have a picnic." I said trying to sound confident. "Or we could still go to a restaurant. I just figured you would prefer this."
She stared at me with that same confused expression she had worn after I bandaged up her side. I wondered why she was so confused.
"It's perfect." Her voice was suddenly quieter, more uncertain.

"Are you okay?" I asked and she nodded. "Okay then let's go."
I thought for a brief second about offering her my hand but was unsure how that would go over. Instead I gestured for her to go ahead before falling in stride with her.
'Coward,' Brooke grumbled irritably.
I ignored this knowing he wanted to feel her touch as much as I did.
We talked for hours until the quarter moon was high in the sky. In our circle of trees with no other light, the moon and stars shone brightly. The air smelled sweet and damp, as if rain was not far off, but the cloudless sky shone with millions of wonders untold.
As we lay only a foot apart and watch, we talked about things of little relevance. Learning our favorite foods and colors, allergies or embarrassing stories. I wished I could stay with her, like that, forever. I knew, however that Tyler was waiting for her, and this perfect moment couldn't last forever.
Just as I thought this my phone pinged with a message from Rowan.
"Avrily went to bed and Tyler wanted to go home so Ro took him back to your place." I informed Myra.
"Ty," Myra sat up looking around as if the darkness had suddenly taken on a new meaning.
"Let's go." I said sliding off before offering her my hand. It was time to get back to reality. I would probably have been disappointed if she hadn't taken my hand unthinkingly. Once she was down she slid her hand away nervously, but I would take what I could get.
At her apartment complex I walked her to her door. After a second of hesitation she met my eyes. It lasted only a couple seconds, but that was a record so far.
"Thank you, I had a good time." She said lookin back at our feet.

"Thank you for coming."

"I-I need to go." Myra said, taking a step away from me.

"Of course." I smiled gently down at her. "Tell Tyler I said hi and next time we can do something together the three of us."

She hesitated frowning. She studied my face as if to find an ulterior meaning to these words.

Finally she nodded slowly before ducking her head and unlocking the door. I couldn't help but notice she moved as if she was expecting to be attacked any second.

'I want to kill whoever hurt mate.' Brooke hissed.

'Me too, but she needs us here more then she needs vengeance right now.' I sighed feeling the repetitive nature of this conversation growing.

'I know.' He sighed, responding to both my words and unspoken annoyance. 'I'm sorry.'

'It's your nature.' I shrugged as I headed back to the car. I wasn't going home though. Tonight I would watchover and be sure no harm came to my family.

Chapter 10

Steam

Over the next two weeks I took both Myra and Tyler out regularly. Myra was often smiling and even laughing in front of me. She had the most beautiful laugh. On our third date, after sitting and watching Ty play at the park, I offered her my hand to help her up. This time was different though, because she didn't let go.

Tyler loved playing with Avrily and Rowan and Myra were becoming good friends as well. They took the kids out regularly. Sometimes Zane and I joined them when we weren't too busy working.

It was Saturday May 10th and I was at the cafe a block away from Myra's apartment. We were supposed to meet up, but she was over an hour late and I was getting worried.

'We would know if someone came for them, right?' Brooke asked nervously.

'Yeah, I mean of course. But we should go check in anyway.' I replied fighting off my anxiety.

"Who is it?" Myra asked when I knocked. Her voice sounded off but I wasn't sure why.

"It's Richard." I responded as I felt my self relax as her scent got closer.

Then the door opened and Myra appeared before me looking slightly nervous. Her long hair was in a messy ponytail and her cheeks were flushed. Her eyes seemed glazed and her brow was damp. She looked sick. Still beautiful, always beautiful, but unwell.

"I'm so sorry." Myra frowned concerned. "Tyler had a fever and has been up all night. I just completely forgot.

I'm sorry."
"You don't look like you feel very good either." I frowned.
I couldn't help but notice that she barely flinched when I reached out to feel her forehead.
"You're burning up you should be laying down." I stepped forward and she moved back allowing me in.
"I will, but Ty needs some water and..." She started.
"Go lay down, I'll get him some." I looked down at her, wiping a stray strand of hair off her face. "Get some rest."
I guided her to her room and motion for her to lay down. Reluctantly she proceeded to do so.
"I'll be right back." I walked out and got Tyler some water.
After checking on him I brought water and Tylenol to Myra.
"Why are you doing this?" She asked awkwardly, "You don't have too."
"I want to, I like taking care of you guys." I smiled at her.
"Why?" She asked again.
I sat next to her on the bed with a sigh.
'Tell her.' Brooke pleaded.
'What? That I'm completely in love with her? She would flip out.'
"Does it really matter?" I asked out loud, brushing my fingers across her warm cheek.
"It does to me, I'm curious."
Was it my imagination or did she lean into my touch. That thought sent a shiver of joy through my entire being and I couldn't help but grin widely at her.
"Haven't you heard curiosity killed the cat?" I asked.
To my surprise she rolled her eyes. "Firstly that was stupidity, curiosity was framed. Secondly I'm not a cat, I'm a wolf, much more dangerous."
I laughed then, without thinking about it, bent down and

kissed her forehead. She gasped almost silently but by the way she closed her eyes I knew she felt it too. The electric shock of energy that left my lips tingling with anticipation.

"Get some sleep." I said again, grinning stupidly at her. The next two days I stayed. I slept on the couch and took care of them both the best I could. I had Logan bring me clothes, soap and my toothbrush. Zane came by daily dropping off any paperwork I needed to do.

Day three Tyler wanted to watch a movie but it was unplugged. After getting shocked a couple times I felt some behind me and looked up.

Myra looked much better then she had the day before as she grinned down at me. The way she bit her lip made me think she was trying not to laugh.

"Need some help down there?" Her hand flinched as if wanting to reach out to touch me.

I knew the feeling, ever since I kissed her forehead every inch of separation seemed torturous.

"You look better today," I observed.

"I feel better, thank you," she admitted before cocking her head at the scorch Mark on the bottom of my green long sleeve shirt.

"I'm not great with electronics." I admitted with a shrug.

"I get it, everybody has their weakness." She stepped aside motioning for me to move. I did.

"Oh yeah? What's yours?"

As I expected she froze, but only for a second. To my surprise though, she did eventually answer.

"Tungsten." She finally replied as she stood back up and facing me.

"What?" I asked, thoroughly confused.

She held out both her hands showing me the scars that encircled her wrists. I had seen them before but still I used the excuse to reach out and take her hands rubbing my thumbs over the scars.

"It's the only metal I can't melt." She shrugged.

It was then I realized exactly what she was telling me, and how much it meant. She had just told me the only way to hold her captive. She trusted me not to share this information, or use it myself.

Without thinking I moved my right hand to her cheek and bent down kissing her lightly on the lips. The second I realized what I had done I expected her to slap me, or at least pull away. I did not expect her to wrap her arms around my neck and stand on her toes to pull me closer. She tasted sweet and smoky at the same time, it was intoxicating.

"Yuck," Tyler said, sounding truest horrified.

Myra jumped back shocked, raising her fingers to her lips.

"I'm sorry," She said quickly before walking away.

I finished turning on the movie before following her back to her room.

"Why are you sorry?" I asked walking over to where she stood facing away from me.

"I'm not good for you, I shouldn't have let that happen." She shook her head.

I spun her so she was facing me with her back to a wall.

"Don't say that. You are exactly what I need in my life" I said stepping closer to her. "You are the fire to my ice." I chuckled at my own lame joke.

Her fair skin was flushed pink and her warm brown eyes met mine effortlessly, something I had worked hard for. A pained smile spread across her face and I wanted to make it better.

I stepped forward pressing her back against the wall then I laid my left hand on the wall next to her head, far enough up to make sure I didn't scare her. I was learning what her boundaries were. What she could and could not handle.

"Do you know what you get when you mix fire and ice?"

She asked breathless as she stared up into my own intense gaze.

"Steam..." I whispered, in my low husky voice.

I lifted my right hand to run my fingers across her cheek. She let out a low involuntary gasp as sparks erupted on my skin where I touched her and I knew she felt it too. Over the past weeks the mate bond was getting stronger than ever.

She closed her eyes reveling in the moment for a second before biting down hard on her lip.

"A puddle..." She gasped, sliding under my arm and walking away wiping at her tears as they slid freely down her cheeks.

I watched her go, with a sad sigh. We had come so far but I had to break through her walls if I was going to save her. Save everyone.

I stuck my hands into my pockets then followed her back out to the living room.

Chapter 11

Let Me In

'Hey Rich, how's it going?' Zane's chocolate brown wolf came to sit on my left.

I huffed a reply laying my head back down on my front paws. We were in the clearing with the trampoline and it was after midnight. The moon was a mear sliver in the sky but the stars shone as brightly as ever.

It had been a whole week since I had kissed Myra in the living room. While she wasn't avoiding me completely, she had managed to avoid being alone with me. This time however it wasn't her fear of me that made her push me away. She knew she was safe with me. It was her fear of us that challenged me now.

She knew we were meant for each other. I know she felt that, but she is too afraid to try again. I don't blame her. She went through hell the last time she was close to someone.

Logan's golden red wolf came and sat on my right.

'Richard, talk to us.' Logan gently, his tail brushing my hip.

'I thought once she realized we were mates she would trust me.' I sighed and Brooke whined quietly, 'But she is fight more than ever. I don't get it, she knows I won't hurt her.'

'Maybe it's more about Tyler then herself.' Zane sighed, allowing himself to fall to his stomach.

'That's irrational. I have shone no threat to him, I try to be good to him.' I snapped, pinning my ears back.

'A mothers love can be irrational.' Zane shot me a look.

He looked like he was about to say something else but we were interrupted by Rowan breaking into our link.

'Logan! Trisha's water broke, Layla is taking her to the

pack hospital.'

We all stood and Zane and I looked and Logan who stood looking scared even in wolf form.

'Go!' I snapped at his back leg forcing him to move. Then he was gone in a flash.

'Oh, and Rich. Myra's blowing up your phone. Do you want me to answer?' Rowan asked.

'Yeah, I'm on my way.' I said as I took off.

I could hear Zane right behind me but I couldn't think of that. All I could think about was Myra. Something had to be wrong, for her to be calling me. What if she was hurt, what if Tyler was hurt? I picked up my pace and Zane fell behind.

'Everything is okay, but you should get here quickly.' Rowan's voice seemed choked. I couldn't tell if she was trying not to laugh, or cry.

'I'm here.' I responded as I bolted up to the house.

Rowan walked outside and rolled her eyes placing her hands on her hips. "You can't hold the phone in the form, genius."

'Oops.'

She looked away as I quickly changed throughout on a pair of basketball shorts.

"You boys have it so easy." Rowan rolled her eyes, handing me the phone.

"Hey Myra. Everything okay?" I gasped ignoring her.

"Mr. Richard?" I breathed a sigh of relief as Tyler's voice came over the phone.

"Hey Ty. How are you doing buddy? Where's your mommy?" I asked as I sat down on the steps.

"She's mad I stoled her phone and locked the door." Tyler admitted sheepishly.

Now that I listened closer I thought I could hear Myra banging on the door.

"Ty that's not a very good thing to do buddy. Why did you

do it?" I asked calmly.

"I miss you. I want you to read me a nigh-night story again." His voice was quiet but the banging in the background had stopped.

I wondered what Myra thought of what she was hearing. I knew she could hear everything if she was trying hard enough. With that thought in mind I took a second to plan my answer.

Finally I took a deep breath and spoke. "I know buddy I miss you too. I have just been busy with work this week." I hated lying to him but he was too young to understand and I wouldn't pin the blame on Myra. I would rather take the fall.

He was quiet for a long time. When he did speak it sounded like he was crying. "It's because you don't want me isn't it..."

I almost started crying right then.

"No baby boy. You're my buddy." I hesitated then decided I had to be honest here, "I love you Tyler, and I would do anything to be with you right now."

"Then come be here." He cried, "It's not too far away."

"I'm so sorry Tyler. I wish I could." I felt so helpless. I wanted to wrap my arms around the little boy and comfort him. All I could do was listen to him crying.

"How about this? I'll ask your mom and see if I can come tuck you in tonight." I submitted.

"O-ok-Kay." He sniffled.

"Tyler I need you to know this has nothing to do with you. I love you and only want you to be happy. I need you to say sorry to your mommy and give her phone back though. Okay?" I spoke gently while trying to maintain some assertion in my tone.

"Yes, sir." Tyler said with a more even voice then he had before. "I love you too Richard."

My heart swelled in my chest, and broke at the same time,

as I hung up the phone. I sat staring at the small black object in my hands replaying his last words over and over in my mind.

I knew the days I had stayed there while they were sick had taken a toll on me. I missed tucking Tyler in and seeing them both every morning. I missed taking care of them. What I hadn't expected was for it to have affected him too. He missed me as well.

I sighed and stared down at the phone. I couldn't decide whether I was more happy that he had bonded with me as well, or sad that that bond was hurting him now. I sighed again laying my face in my palms.

Suddenly a small hand gripped my shoulder. "It'll all work out Rich. You have to believe that."

I nodded slowly. "I have to talk to her."

"I'll see if Avrily can go over for a play date. You can give her a ride right?" When I looked up Rowan was smiling mischievously at me.

She pulled out her phone and after a few tapa of the screen she put it to her ear.

While I was still debating whether or not I should stop her she started talking again. "Hey Myra I have a favor to ask of you?"

"What's going on?" Myra sounded tired.

Brooke whimpered in my head, he never did much more than that these days.

"Trish is having the baby and I want to go to the hospital. I could leave Avrily with Zane but she has been begging to play with Ty." Rowan said in an exhausted concerned voice.

"Of course she can come over. Honestly I think Ty could use the pick me up."

"Oh thank you so much! Rich will bring her over, I'm desperate to get to the hospital." Rowan said excitedly.

"Oh... okay." Myra said, sounding unsure again. "Let me

know how it goes with Trish."
"Of course! Thank you so much! I'll let you know if I can still do coffee tomorrow morning also."
"Sounds good Ro." Myra sounded happy again.
"Okay bye!" Rowan hung up the phone and grinned down at me.
"I didn't know you were so anxious to get to the hospital." I mused.
She rolled her eyes waving a dismissive hand at me. "Are you kidding, labor takes hours and Trish won't be ready to see us for even longer. I'm going to take a nap."
I laughed, "I never knew you were such a good actress."
"Oh hun. I know you didn't." She grinned at me before skipping up the steps her blonde curls bouncing behind her. For such a tiny innocent looking girl, there were times I wondered if maybe she was more dangerous than I was.
Avrily burst out the door, "Let's go let's go!" She cheered excitedly.
"Okay princess, lets go."
I reached in the door grabbing my keys. Then I slid on a red T-shirt and some flip flops.
Reaching down I grabbed Avrilys hand and led her to the car. I knew I had to talk to her, and now I had the means to do that. Only problem was I had no clue what I was going to say.

Chapter 12

Running Again

The second my knuckles hit the door it flew open. Tyler bolted out wrapping his tiny arms tightly around my legs. Quickly I crouched down hugging the child closely to me. I felt more complete with him there, I had missed him so much. Only one person was missing.

As I looked up to search for her, I noticed the pained expression on her face. I could feel her inner turbulence as she battled to figure out what she was supposed to do. I knew she had never thought it would hurt Tyler so bad to push me away.

"Um, hello?! Ty-ty I'm here to play." Avrily announced stomping her foot and crossing her arms.

I couldn't help but chuckle as Tyler looked up embarrassed.

"Are you leaving?" He asked me desperately.

I made eye contact with Myra silently asking her the same thing. When she didn't respond I took the initiative, "No I'm going to hang out and talk to mommy for a bit."

"Okay. I'm gonna go play, don't leave!" Tyler commanded.

"Yes sir." I said attempting to look as serious as possible. Out of the corner of my eye I saw Myra crack a smile. Then the kids ran inside heading back towards Tyler's room. I entered the apartment closing the door slowly behind me. I met Myra's gaze for a split second before her warm brown eyes fell to the floor. I followed as she headed into the kitchen silently.

She started fidgeting with stuff on the counter so I slid onto a bar stool to wait.

'Damn it Rich, say something!' Brooke snapped at me.
'No. She needs a minute to gather her thoughts before this conversation. I'm not going to rush her.' I responded smoothly.
Brooke was much more aware and active back in her presence.
"I'm sorry about this morning." Myra finally murmured reluctantly.
"It was nice to hear from him." I admitted with a shrug, "I missed him... I missed you both."
"I know," she sighed, turning to look at me. "I got an offer, I didn't... still don't know what to do though."
I froze confused this wasn't what I had been expecting.
"An offer on what?" I finally asked.
"A safe place for people like us. Where we can be with others similar to us and fit in. I know that others with our particular abilities are rare but there are other more common ones." She explained this quietly. She frowned as if she wasn't sure she believed what she was saying.
I on the other hand had heard the speech before and felt my anxiety rising. I couldn't believe Azreal had gotten a hold of her so soon. She hadn't excepted the mate bond yet. What if she believed this load of lies over me.
I nodded dumbly unsure what else to do.
"Apparently a lot of wolves with abilities and their families have formed this community. It's their own pack." She said still unsure.
"It's not real Myra..." I finally said after a long pause.
"How do you know?" She snapped, crossing her arms.
I knew how badly she wanted to believe this. Hell, I had wanted to also and I already had a pack I was devoted to when I was told.
"It's the same lie I almost fell for, and trust me it's dangerous." I pleaded nonverbally that she would heed my warning.

"Why should I believe you. It could be different." She
sounded as if she was trying to convince herself as much
as she was me.
"Because I know within three guesses who told you about
it." I admitted sadly. "Zachary Hicks, Damon Smith, or
Azrael Black."
She sighed defeated as she sat slowly on another stool.
"Zachary..." She admitted. "What do they want?"
"Warriors they can control. They believe werewolves are
a superior species and should conquer and imprison
humans..." I felt glad that she seemed to believe me.
However the pain I felt, knowing all she wanted was to fit
in, wasn't only mine.
She nodded both unsurprised and unphased. I once again
realized that with what she had been through almost
nothing surprised her. With that thought in mind I was
shocked when she suddenly gasped and stared at the
phone in her hand.
Her eyes widened, her heart raced, and her breathing was
ragged gasps. She threw her phone hard against the wall
and I watched, shocked, as it busted into several pieces.
Suddenly she was crying. She slid down onto the floor
pulling her legs tightly against herself.
For a second I just stared unsure how to react, but then
Brooke took over rushing to Myra's side defensively.
"What's wrong." His words escaped my mouth in a low
growl.
At first she just sobbed and I sat next to her wrapping my
arms around her. Her small form trembled as sobs racked
her body.
"He's working with them I'm sure. I was so stupid!"She
sobbed.
This only confused me more. What on earth was she
talking about.
"Hey it'll be okay." I soothed running my fingers through

her hair.

We sat like that for a long minute. Until suddenly she took a deep breath and pulled away. She disappeared down the hall coming back with a duffle bag and my heart jumped. There were already some clothes in it, and I watched horrified as she started shoving in non perishable food and reusable water bottles.

I stepped in front of her crossing my arms stubbornly over my chest. "What do you think you are doing?"

"I told them what territory I was in, by now Victor knows for sure. I knew I recognised that scent yesterday..." She trailed off the last part not meant to be out loud.

"What scent?" I asked, frowning at the bag.

She stared at me for a minute before shaking her head, "It doesn't matter, we have to leave."

"You are not going anywhere." I stated firmly.

"Yes I am."

She glared at me in the most annoyingly stubborn way, only she could. I sighed, knowing arguing wouldn't work.

'You can't just let her go!' Booke screamed in my head.

'No dip sherlock. Anything useful to say?' I snapped in response, silently wishing he would shut up again.

'If she's leaving, we are going with her.' Brooke stated confidently.

The idea was painful and I couldn't help but grimace. On one hand everyone I knew and loved lived here, I didn't want to leave them. However on the other hand maybe Logan's fears of my ability causing the pack trouble didn't have to come to fruition.

A look of concern suddenly filled Myra's eyes, and she reached up placing her hand on my cheek. I knew she was feeling my pain, and in return I could feel her confusion. As her hand touched my face I realized that I actually could leave for her and Tyler.

"If you go, I'm going with you." I stated confidently.

"You can't do that, you're the Beta." She gasped, "You can't just leave."

I slowly warped my arms loosely around her waist as her hand slid down to my chest. "Try to stop me."

"Logan won't let you." She frowned, refusing to meet my gaze.

"I'm the rightful alpha, he can't stop me. Not that he would try." I added the last part to comfort myself. I hated the idea of having to overrule Logan, though I knew I could.

"You were adopted, you don't have alpha blood?" She stated this like a question.

"The alpha adopted me and saw me completely as his son, he passed the leadership to me." I admitted, "It wasn't until weeks later I passed it to Logan. Since I was given it by someone as they died, it still technically is mine until I die."

I tried my best to explain but the confused expression on her face was proof I wasn't doing very well.

I sighed, "Are we leaving?"

She frowned, staring down at the bag. "I don't want to drag you into this."

I rolled my eyes before using two fingers to lift her chin so she had to look at me. "Are we running?"

Brooke snarled, he hated the idea of running away from anything.

Myra met my gaze then nodded slowly, "I have to, but you dont Richard."

"Let me help grab your stuff. We will take my car, so you can bring more. I have cash and a burner phone at home, untraceable. We will take Avery home, grab my stuff, then go to a place I know. It'll be safe. Leave your phone here. Do you have your money?" I asked, going over a mental checklist.

Myra nodded. Then to my surprise she threw her arms

around my neck burying her face in my neck.
"Thank you." She said, sounding slightly defeated.
I held her for a second before responding. "You are going to be okay. I won't let anyone near either of you."
After a couple minutes we pulled apart.
"Okay," I said cupping her cheek in my hand, "Go get blankets, more clothes, and a couple books and toys for Ty in the car."
Myra nodded then rushed down the hall.
'This is ridiculous, she is safest here.' Brooke whined.
'She doesn't trust that and you can't blame her for that.' I retorted
'Then talk her into believing it.'
'And risk her disappearing alone into the night?' Brooke and I both winced, 'No way.'
'Then we are really leaving...' Brooke sighed.
'Temporarily, think of it as a vacation.'
Brooke whimpered quietly and I sighed. Then I got to work collecting more food and filling jugs of water.

Chapter 13

On the Road

In only two hours we had packed up my car, dropped Avery off with Zane, and left a letter for Logan explaining the best I could. I told Zane everything I knew when I dropped off Avery.

I had been prepared to plead with him to pick up my slack while I was gone. Of course Zane had told me to go, do what I needed and come back. He promised to cover for me and slipped me a burner cell.

"It has our numbers." He smiled sadly, "We all figured this might happen at some point. Logan won't be upset. Call if you need us."

I couldn't help the burning guilt though. I felt especially guilty since Logan would have extra pressure with his new baby. I hated adding to his burden, but I couldn't risk losing my mate or my son.

I surprised myself thinking the words, my son, as I looked at Tyler in the rear view mirror. I smiled at the child as his head lolled to the side in his sleep. I shifted my gaze to his mother. Myra stared out the window looking sorrowfully at the forest flying by.

I could only imagine the pain, fear, and guilt that fought in her own mind. Her inner turmoil had to be as bad if not worse than mine. I wanted to ease her conscious, tell her she wasn't alone anymore.

'Say something charming.' Brooke suggested.

'I haven't exactly had a chance to plan something.' I hissed silently.

I had no clue what to say or do and I could feel Brooke rolling his eyes as his deep sigh echoed around my head.

'Helpless, worse than a newborn pup…' He muttered, 'Ridiculous.'

Okay, so I didn't have a ton of experience with women. In fact I had spent most of my life focusing on controlling and strengthening my power over water. I didn't have much time for dating.

However I felt his words were still incredibly harsh, and definitely uncalled for.

'Watch it.' I snapped defensively.

'Let me talk for a second.' He sighed.

Reluctantly I obliged.

He reached out our right hand intertwining our hand with hers, "It's going to be okay Myra."

She looked down at our hands then at me. A tentative smile spread over her face, but she didn't pull away.

"I'm sorry you got dragged into this." She sounded so guilty, and the wave of sorrow that washed over me would have knocked me off my feet if I wasn't already sitting. "I never wanted to take you away from your family."

"You are my family now." The response was both Brooke and I, and completely automatic. Neither one of us had to think about a response even for a second. "Don't get me wrong I love them like brothers and sisters, but… you are my mate. I'll do anything for you and they get that."

She blushed the blood in her cheeks accentuating the red in her hair. She was stunning and I couldn't help but smile back.

Myra turned away looking back out the window. We had come so far from where we had begun, but it still stung when she shut down and turned away. I wished she would tell me what she was thinking, what we were running from. Normally within a week mates were marked and there were no more secrets. I had known from the start that these weren't normal circumstances. That didn't stop me from wishing she would talk to me.

'She's too stubborn and strong for her own good.' Brooke grumbled.

'That's why she's still alive.' I reminded him.

'I know.' He purred.

'What's with that reaction?' I ask mistafide.

'Our mate is amazing.' He sighed happily.

I chuckled out loud and shook my head.

"What?" Myra asked, frowning.

The way her lips puckered slightly, made me want to kiss her. The cute little v that formed between her eyes took my breath away. My attraction to her had only grown unbearably strong in the past months.

"Brookes just being bipolar." I forced a smile.

Her returning smile was half hearted. She glanced into the back seat again.

"Thank you," She said cautiously. "This is much easier on him than running, or even me carrying him. He's getting too big for that anyway."

She frowned as though that thought troubled her more than she wanted to admit.

I nodded then asked the question that had been nagging at me, "You never told me what scent."

"I had a rough day at work yesterday so I went on a run. Rowan had Ty so I figured it was fine but…" she frowned out the window. "I crossed a scent that wasn't from this pack. At first I couldn't place it but last night I had nightmares about Tyler's dad and his pack.

"He would never threaten a large pack like yours but he would sneak in. He is determined to get to us." Her voice shook and she frowned, clearly frustrated about it.

"When we go back you should think about staying at the pack house. Far out of his reach." I said trying to hide my anger.

'Why can't he just leave them alone?' I groaned angrily.

'Let him come…' Brooke snarled.

I sighed and stared out the windshield.

"Do you think it could be possible?" She asked quietly as she stared out her window.

'What's she talking about?' Brooke asked.

'Ummm…'

'You don't have a clue do you?' He sighed, 'Smooth.'

'You don't know either genius.' I snapped, wishing there was a mute button somewhere.

"What's possible?" I finally asked.

"A pack of people like us. A safe haven where we could be… normal." She whispered.

"I think it could be, but it would take someone very powerful to lead such a pack. Someone would have to start it from scratch. It would be especially hard because most wolves with any abnormal power are forced to hide." I frowned, "Even gifts as common as Psychics are hunted by alphas who want their power.

"Then there are the scams that make us all reluctant to believe in such a place. It would be hard work, and a lot of it."

"Sounds like you have thought a lot about it." She commented glancing at me.

I shrugged. Everyone had dreams right. Mine however would be impossible on my own. Even if Myra helped me, we couldn't do it alone. We would need a shadow. Shadows were nearly impossible to find and pretty rare. Let me explain a light. A shadow is a wolf who can seemingly vanish in thin air. They are difficult to find and even harder to sneak up on. However they can sense the powers of other wolves and are often drawn to them. The problem is when all the alphas went power crazy Shadow wolves were their first target. They wanted to force these wolves to lead them to other powerful wolves. In return wolves with other gifts often killed Shadows at first sight. Any that survived learned to run from any power they sensed.

Therefore two very powerful wolves would have a terrible time trying to locate a shadow. Much less get it to talk to us.

I sighed quietly and pushed down on the gas a little harder. I wanted to get to our destination before sunset.

dmittions

Late that night I parked in the driveway of a small, one story two bedroom, cottage deep in the woods. It was on our neighboring packs territory, but I had asked Zane to let them know we would be here. It was one of several cabins often used as safe houses for our packs. Normally they were just places for mother's and children when there was a battle.

We had several on our territory for them and they maintained several for us. The theory was that most enemies didn't look beyond the borders of whatever pack they were attacking. It worked well and had saved many people over generations.

"Are you sure this is safe?" Myra whispered, glancing around desperately. "Other wolves were here only a couple hours ago!"

I understood her panic. She had been a rogue for a long time, and rogues are far from welcomed with most packs.

"Yes I'm sure. Grace, the alpha, knew we were coming and probably just restocked the cabin." I responded, reaching over to squeeze her hand gently. "I'm not going to let anything happen to you Myra."

I must have said these words a million times, but I would say them a million more if that's what it took for her to believe me.

She turned towards me smiling cautiously.

"Can we get out?" Tyler groaned from the back.

The past several hours he had been trying to entertain himself with the limited amount of kids stuff I had in my car. I made a mental note to get more.

Worry flickered in Myra's eyes for a second, but then she met mine again and said, "Yeah, it's okay. Just stay close to the house."

Then we opened our door and I quickly got into the back helping Tyler unbuckle his car seat. After Tyler ran a few paces he shifted into his wolf. The red sable puppy bound and leaped running circles around the house and darting in and out of the trees.

I couldn't help but chuckle as I watched him. I could remember having that much energy, as well as not having complete control of your wolf. The first two to three years a child shifts they go through at least four times the amount of clothing as others their age.

"Again?" Myra sighed leaning against the car next to me. "This kid is going to be out of clothing soon if he doesn't calm down."

I shrugged, "Boys will be boys and pups will be pups. I'll get him some new clothes next time I head into town."

Myra surprised me then by smiling and laying her head against my arm. She was so much shorter than I was, so much more pale. She was by appearance my polar opposite.

However she was strong and brave, kind and nurturing, and once you get to see past her walls she just wants to be cared for. The way she watched Tyler made my heart ache knowing m, hoping, one day she would watch our pups the same way.

As I glanced down I noticed something for the first time. On the left side and the base of her neck was a bite mark. Someone had tried to mark her as his own. Anger burned in my chest andBrooke growled lowly.

'She's already marked? Nobody does that. That's beyond criminal. If the council find out he would be beheaded.' Brooke snarled.

'Why is it so jagged and ripped?' I asked him silently.

With one hand I reached down rubbing my fingers lightly over the scar. Myra flinched, pain flashing in her eyes, and I quickly allowed my hand to slip down and around her waist. I pulled her tighter into my side and kissed the top of her head.

'Because she fought it. Being marked by someone who isn't your mate is excruciating and leaves a lingering pain until it's fixed.' Brooke informed me sadly. 'It's been forbidden and considered a capital crime for years.'

"I'm sorry." Myra interrupted our conversation.

Unsure what to say I gave her a light squeeze, "You did nothing wrong Myra."

"I should have stopped him." She rubbed her wrists nervously.

After a short pause I asked, "Why didn't he get burned?" At first I thought she wouldn't reply. We watched as Tyler darted towards a tree and jumped as if trying to climb it.

I chuckled as he tumbled back the short distance to the ground, clearly not hurt.

"By then he had found a way to subdue the flames and silence Em." Myra whispered so quietly I barely heard her.

"What do you mean?" I asked, trying to mask my anger.

Myra sighed, "Em doesn't respond to cold well. If my body temperature drops to low she kind of goes dormant. I lose my abilities, she doesn't talk to me, I…" She hesitated, "I basically become human."

I nodded, "That must be terrifying."

She shrugged, "I got used to it after a while. He used it frequently as a punishment and threatened it to get me to do what he wanted. If I refused completely he… he started threatening to kill Tyler."

I stiffened and clenched my jaw.

"I was stupid enough to think he wouldn't kill his own

son…" Her voice trailed.

"That scar on his shoulder was because you weren't following orders?" I asked quietly, I hoped at the tone the disgust was still obvious.

"Yeah. I messed up. I refused to set fire to a family's house. The mom had apparently rejected his advances. Then the father refused to force her to participate in Victors games." She shrugged, as if talking about him being with married women while forcing her to be with him was normal.

I noticed she rarely spoke the dirtbags name. He may have been Tyler's biological father, but he had no place in their lives.

"That's disgusting." I spat, unable to hide my contempt. She shrugged, "That's Victor. He's the alpha, he gets what he wants when he wants it or else."

Suddenly she looked concerned again. It struck me that what Victor wanted right now was her and Tyler. He didn't care about the mate bond clearly. This time though he was biting off more than he could chew. I would destroy him. I would protect my family with everything I had.

I squeezed her shoulder again, sighing contentedly as she leaned against me finally.

"How about we head on in and get dinner ready?" I suggested, "It's been a long day for all of us."

I felt her nod slowly.

Chapter 15

Safe Haven

As I walked past the open door to Myra's room I saw her standing and staring out the window. Her back was to me, her long strawberry blonde hair waved down her back. She wore pajama shorts and a tank top.

She stood so still, staring out as if waiting for someone to walk out of the trees.

I walked up behind her and brushed my fingers down her bare arms. She stiffened momentarily but quickly relaxed and even leaned back into me.

"You are safe here." I whispered into her hair.

I couldn't help breathing in her smell. Fresh rain in a forest, it was made for me. She took a shuddering breath and I realized that she had been holding her breath. I listened as her heart beat faster and I felt the heat as blood rushed into her cheeks.

She turned to face me and we were only inches apart. I wanted her so bad. My skin was on fire. I needed her touch. I slowly reached out and cupped her cheek. Then I bent closing the space between us.

She returned the kiss desperately, wrapping her arms around my neck and pulling me tighter to her.

I reached down with my right arm sweeping her legs out from under her and cradling her to my chest without breaking our kiss.

Hours later I laid on the bed with Myra still next to me. I wrapped my arms securely around her body. She wore only my dark grey T-shirt that hung loosely around her small frame. Her scent engulfed me and I had never been more happy in my life. I sighed contentedly.

"Richard?" Myra's voice was hushed but content.

"Yes?" I asked as I kissed the top of her head.

Instead of responding she shifted so she was hovering over me. She kissed her way down to the soft spot on the nape of my neck.

I shuddered in anticipation. Then I gasped as her canines sunk into the soft skin. Suddenly I could sense her even more then before. I wanted more though as she ran her tongue over the spot. I wanted to mark her back.

She sighed happily, still straddling me but she sat back. The only thing separating us was the thin fabric of my boxers. She shifted her hair exposing her own neck. Her eyes glistened desperately.

"Please fix it?" She bit her lip as if concerned I would say no.

I sat up slowly and kissed the scar that was already in place. I had seen it before. However, the torn edges that showed her struggle against that monster still infuriated me. Now she was asking me to cure her from the constant pain. The punishment of being marked by someone other than your mate.

I bit her quickly marking her as mine. I winced as I felt the wave pain she had endured a second before it faded to nothing.

She gasped in surprise before sighing blissfully. She relaxed into my embrace.

I ran my tongue over the mark sealing it permanently. She was free of him and his mark forever.

"Thank you." Myra sighed resting her head on my shoulder again.

"My pleasure." I chuckled happier than I had ever imagined possible.

I was surprised when an unfamiliar fear started slowly burning in my gut. It took me longer than it should have to realize, it wasn't my fear. Now that we had marked each other even the smallest hint of emotion that could mean danger would be shared.

"What's wrong? Why are you worried?" I pulled her back so I could see her eyes.

She slid off my lap and sat next to me. She wrapped her arms around her knees.

"What happens now?" She asked, staring down.

I slid my arms around and pulled her back on my lap. I cradled her into my chest not willing to let her go yet.

"That's for us to decide, together. I'll go first. I love you Myra and I don't want to be separated from you ever again." I comforted her by running my hand through her strawberry blonde hair.

Her joy at those words was overwhelming. I couldn't help the thrill I got knowing she liked that.

"I love you too, but." She hesitated, "It's not just me."

'Tyler, she's worried we won't accept Tyler' Brooke explained while I fought back a wave of jealousy.

'That's not logical.' I replied. 'I have shown nothing but patients and kindness to him.'

'Remember what Zane said about a mothers love being irrational? I suspect she wants to believe you love him but she can't until you tell her point blank that you accept and embrace him.'

I shifted so she had to meet my gaze and spoke with the assurance of the alpha I was meant to be.. "I know Myra, I love that little boy more than I ever imagined possible."

Her relief washed over both of us like a tidal wave. I gingerly brush my thumb across her cheek.

"When I say I love you, I mean every part of you. Tyler is a part of who you are. If he will have me I would proudly call him my son." I said honestly, watching as tears filled her eyes.

Suddenly she threw herself against me kissing me hungrily. I chuckled, laying back and pulling her with me. She moaned blissfully as I rolled so I was hovering over her.

"Patients love. I have to get something first." I murmured into her neck.

"Hurry." She growled nibbling at my ear.

I groaned happily once again claiming my mate all to myself. Myra was mine nobody else had any rights to this perfect woman.

"Mommy!" Tylers scream from across the hall reminded me that I was wrong.

I threw on a pair of shorts before following Myra as she rushed to Tylers room.

"What is it?" Brooke's growl escaped through my lips.

It was then I realized how close I was to shifting. My gaze darted around the room looking for the threat.

The dresser and desk were still against the walls to my left and right. The small bed now occupied by Myra who was crading Tylers trembling form.

"I'm sorry." She said instinctively. "He just had a nightmare. Settle down Brooke."

He did, allowing me to regain composure. I sighed running my hand over my hair. I slowly walked forward and sat facing them.

"You okay Ty?" I asked, reaching out to gently wipe a tear off his cheek.

I felt the same stab of pain I always did as he flinched away from my hand.

"I'm sorry." He choked, tears filling his eyes again.

"You never have to apologize for being scared, Tyler. It's natural and necessary to survive." I said calmly.

"Really?" Tyler asked looking up curiously.

He used the back of his hand to wipe his cheeks.

"Of course." I smiled, glad to have distracted him. "Why do you think a lone wolf will run from a large bear?"

"Because he's not stupid." Tyler said wide eyed.

I chuckled, "See? His fear of the bear is smart, it protects him. Fear can be good. It's when you let it start running your life that you need to work on it."

"Oh," Tyler said as Myra shifted uncomfortably.

I hadn't meant that directed at her, but by her discomfort she had taken it that way.

However, before I could say anything a loud knocking reverberated through the small house. Myra's eyes widened and her embrace around Tyler stiffened.

"Stay here." I commanded quietly.

Panic grew stronger in Myra's eyes as I stood. She shook her head, her eyes pleading with me to stay.

"I'll be right back." I promised.

As I headed down the hall I wondered who in the world would be knocking at the door at one in the morning. On one hand our enemies weren't likely to knock on the door and announce their presents. On the other hand I knew nobody from either pack would come banging on the door at this time.

As I reached the front door I took a deep breath. It was a wolf. His scent was familiar but unknown at the same time. This confused me. I knew I had never smelled this scent but I had to know somebody closely related for it to be so familiar. A sibling or parent.

'A father…' Brooke snarled in the back of my mind.

I tensed preparing to fight as I laid my hand on the door handle.

Chapter 16

The Tracker

With a deep breath I turned the knob cracking the door open. In the doorway stood a fair skinned man with light brown hair and deep brown eyes. He was tall and stocky, built like a tank. He wore tennis shoes, sweatpants, and a tank-top. Also he was soaking wet. It looked as if he had ran through the river to get here.
"Who are you and what are you doing here?" My voice was one step away from a snarl.
"Woah," The man said holding up his hands in a peace gesture. "I just came to talk to Myra."
"Who are you?" I asked again, my voice no longer a hint of a snarl but the real thing.
The stranger frowned, examining me as if unsure how to respond to this simple question.
"Who are you?" He asked, suddenly serious.
His tone and expression had shifted. Up until this point he had seemed like a wandering random wolf. Now he had a calmness and determination that made me uncomfortable. His gaze seemed to see more then anyone else I had ever met before.
Despite this Brooke snarled stepping forward out the door, trying to force the stranger to take a step back. He stood his ground, flinching only slightly.
"Answer my question first." I growled, now less than a foot of distance between us.
"First answer this at least. Are you on her side or his?" He snarled back.
I was so used to towering over people it surprised me when he only stood a couple inches shorter than me.

Despite the difference in height he stubbornly stood his ground.

"Always hers." I snapped.

He laughed relieved, "Oh thank god dude. She has far too many dangerous enemies. If you were against her, that girl would be screwed. Dude you are terrifying." He stepped back.

I stood there dumbfounded by the sudden shift in atmosphere. I was vaguely aware my mouth was hanging open but couldn't seem to figure out how to fix that. I was stunned.

"So is she inside?" He asked, stepping closer again to peer around me.

I shifted automatically to block his view. And held up my hand.

"Who are you?" I asked again.

"Trystan?!" I heard Myra shriek excitedly from behind me.

"Trystan? The twin brother? Trystan?" I asked looking back at her as she ran past me wrapping her arms around his waist.

"What are you doing here?" She asked, suddenly pulling back.

I was fighting jealousy as well as frustration, I was NOT used to being ignored. However I was glad she had thought to put on a pair of pajama pants before coming out. She still wore my T-shirt which calmed me more than I would have expected. My mark was clear on her shoulder since her hair was pulled back. That and the fact I knew my scent was all over her comforted me greatly.

"I had a visit from..." He hesitated looking up at me before continuing in a language I didn't understand. "Un amico comune. Dovevo assicurarmi che fossi al sicuro."

"Stiamo bene. Cosa voleva?" She replied in a shaking voice.

"Voi." He said adamantly.

Myra shuttered and I instinctively stepped towards her.

"What is going on? And sense when do you speak spanish." I asked.

Trystan grinned, "Italian."

"Whatever. How did you find us?" I demanded laying my hand gently on Myra's back.

She leaned into me unconsciously.

"Quanto ne sa?" Trystan said to Myra.

"Everything, except what you can do. That's not my secret to share." Myras responded quietly.

I appreciated the english response.

"Thank you." He said adamantly.

"Duh," She rolled her eyes, then she added seriously.

"You can trust him though."

"Will somebody please tell me what's going on?" I massaged my forehead with my free hand.

"She's telling me I can trust you." Trystan explained.

Pride filled my chest and I smiled down at her. I had worked so hard to prove that I was trustworthy to her. Hearing her say it put me on cloud nine.

"Victor came to my place looking for you a few weeks ago. We had already left, Ally saw him coming. I know I promised not to but I had to find you and make sure you were okay." He explained, seeming suddenly exhausted.

"I don't want you involved..." Myra started.

Trystan laughed humorlessly, "When are you going to get it though that head of yours. I'm your brother, I'm in as deep as you. You could use the help."

"How did you find us though?" I asked for what felt like the millionth time. "I know nobody who knew where we were would tell you. This place isn't on any map, only the two packs that use it know it exists."

Trystan looked uncomfortable but Myra nodded encouragingly.

"I'm a tracker. If I have met somebody and know their scent I can find them no matter how far away they may be." He admitted looking suddenly nervous.

I understood his hesitation, being different was dangerous. I had unknowingly asked him to show his cards before I showed mine.

Taking a deep breath I extended my mind repelling the water from his clothes drying him instantly.

"Hey you didn't set my pants on fire this time." He smiled at Myra who blushed deeply.

"That was Richard, not me. I probably would at least leave you steaming still. He has more control." She admitted, embarrassed.

"More training, you're getting better." I said, earning a smile.

"Wait, you do the whole fire thing too?" Trystan asked shocked.

"No," I said, collecting all of the water from his clothes and forming a massive ball in between us. I froze it solid before allowing it to drop. With the faults and weaknesses I had put in the ball all that survived was a perfect water droplet. "Water."

Myra rolled her eyes, "Show off."

Trystan laughed, "See I knew you were scary. Damn."

"Wait." Myra said, suddenly concerned. "Where is Allison?"

"Oh," Trystan face palmed, "She's going to kill me. She's waiting about a mile away. I didn't want to bring her if I didn't know it was safe."

"Well go get her quickly. Then you guys need to come in. There's a room available for you." Myra said determinedly.

A faint worry spread from her and over me I reached down taking her hand and smiling at her. She calmed quickly, I wondered what she had been worried about.

"Thanks." Trystan said before bolting.

"You don't mind do you?" She asked nervously.

I chuckled, "We will have to share a room now."

She blushed, lifting her face to kiss me deeply.

"Good lord woman. You're going to be the death of me." I gasped after a minute.

She chuckled happily. Then leaned into me and watched the edge of the trees nervously.

"So," I whispered, pulling her closer. "You trust me?"

I couldn't help but remember the first time I had asked and how she had said no. I anxiously waited as she slowly looked up at me. She looked somewhat embarrassed but still happier than I had seen her before.

"Yes, I do." She blushed, the color emphasizing the red in her hair.

I wanted to take her in my arms and never let her go.

From that moment I realized I had a family now. I was no longer fighting to obtain them; they were mine. With that I lifted her up enough that I could devour her succulent lips more easily.

She chuckled, wrapping her legs around my waist. Brooke snarled ravenously and I groaned quietly.

"Dude, that's my sister." Trystan's voice barely registered, but Myra pushing away did clearly.

"Oh leave them alone. Just be happy she finally found her mate, and he accepted her." A tall thin redhead spoke punching Trystan in the arm.

"Ali!" Myra squealed running over to the women.

They embraced and jumped up and down with squeals of delight.

"I told you the new moon park was your safe zone." Allison grinned widely.

"You could have told me why." Myra grumbled.

Alison took no notice of this. Instead she walked up to me and gave me a quick hug.

"It's so good to finally meet you!" She beamed after pulling away. "Don't worry we are going to be just like siblings. Also you will make an amazing Alpha when all of this is past."

"I'm a Beta." I said stunned.

"I know, but that won't last forever." She smiled knowingly. "And the room is perfect."

Then without another word she walked right past me and into the room I had been planning on offering them.

"Sorry," Trystan said awkwardly, "She takes some getting used to."

Myra laughed.

Chapter 17

Explanations

The next morning I woke up to the door creaking open.
"Mommy?" Tyler whispered as he poked his head in.
"Hey bud. Are you hungry?" I asked after verifying that
Myra was still sleeping peacefully.
Tyler nodded with a smile.
I climbed out of bed. I wore only a pair of baggy sweats
but I didn't want to chance waking her up. So I led Tyler
into the kitchen.
It was small but homey. Two walls had light cherry top and
bottom cupboards as well as concrete countertops. The tile
floor was white, not my top choice. The appliances were all
white as well.
Tyler walked to the small table in the middle of the room
and sat down.
"Okay how about some toaster waffles?" I offered.
"Yes please." Tyler nodded vedinantly.
I chuckle before tossing a couple of waffles in the toaster.
"Richard?" Tyler asked quietly.
"Yes?" I asked, trying to ignore the pang of pain from his
nervousness.
"Do you love my mommy?" He asked as I set his plate and
a glass of water on the table.
"I love you both." I responded carefully.
I remembered our first conversation and how he thought
anyone who cared about his mom would hate him. The last
thing I wanted was for him to think I hated him.
"Does that mean you are my new daddy?" He asked,
confused.
With everything he had gone through Tyler seemed so

mature that I often forgot he was still just a child. At only five years old, this must be a really confusing situation for him.

I sighed quietly, trying to decide what to say.

"Do you want me to be, Ty?" I asked after a long pause. Tyler nodded shyly.

I couldn't help but smile brightly at him, but before I could speak Trystan's voice boomed happily through the room.

"Tyler! Goodness, you're getting so big." Trystan walked closer to Ty, too excited about meeting the child to realize the boy's fear.

Tyler, clearly not comfortable with being addressed so directly by a complete stranger, slid off his chair and moved to hide behind me.

I felt bad for Trystan who frowned unhappily, but I couldn't help the joy that Tyler trusted me to protect him.

"He doesn't know you yet Trystan, give the kid a break." Alison said calmly as she walked in. She wore pink yoga pants and a black tank top."I warned you you were going to scare him. You owe me twenty."

"I don't know why you would ever bet against her." Myra said walking in behind them. She still wore the sweats and my T-shirt.

Trystan rolled her eyes, "One of these days I will win."

"So you must be a pretty powerful psychic if you're mates to a tracker, right? From what I have read mates normally have close to the same amount of power." I commented as Myra walked over and started making more waffles.

"You know most psychics can only see whatever path you have chosen right?" Alison asked happily.

"Ally..." Trystan said nervously.

He clearly still didn't trust me enough with details, especially of his mate. I could understand his protectiveness.

"Trystan, I already told you, this is the best way to form the relationship we will have." She glared at him.

Trystan sighed unhappily. I could only imagine the discomfort and turmoil he had to be feeling right now. He placed his arm gently around her waist and looked at me concerned.

I nodded slowly answering her question.

"I can see every possibility and eventuality just by meeting someone once. That's why I sent Myra to you, I knew it was the best option for her." Alison smiled.

"Wow, and I guess I owe you my thanks then." I smiled down at Myra, who moved to stand beside me.

"Why didn't you tell me why you sent me, or that I could trust him though?" She asked Alison, crossing her arms clearly frustrated.

Alison frowned for a second then took a deep breath. "It was something you had to learn on your own for it to be as strong enough to survive the trials of the future."

There was a long heavy silence that fell over the kitchen.

"Woah, that was as foreboding as the Oracle of Delphi." Trystan finally said with a forced laugh.

Everyone stared at him for a moment before we started chuckling. I suddenly remembered Myra saying that Trystan never took anything seriously.

However I now saw that wasn't true. While he eased the tension with a joke I could clearly see a deep concern etched in his expression. Trystan took everything seriously, but he hid it and tried to to help everyone else relax. I could definitely see the benefit of that.

"Oh and by the way, you are going to want a shirt to answer that." Alison told me with an amused grin.

"Answer what?" Just as I said it there was a knock on the door.

Myra chuckled and I rolled my eyes.

Believing Alison all too well I quickly grab a tank top on my way to the door.

"Richard!" Susan beamed at me.

I had known Susan since I had been adopted. We had been friends until she had become obsessed with the idea of us being some kind of power couple. There were several things wrong with the idea, the main one was we were simply not compatible. That made it impossible for us to be mates. Suffice to say, I was glad I had grabbed a shirt.

"I accidentally sent the wrong laundry soap when I ordered the place stocked for you. I figured I just had to fix it myself." She said calmly.

"Thanks." I said taking the soap.

I had learned not to say too much; she tended to take everything as confirmation of a love that didn't exist.

"Anyway I guess I should get back. I have a date. Did you hear I found my mate? I heard you did too." She said awkwardly.

"That's great. I wish you all the best. Thanks again." I said calmly.

She nodded and walked away.

I stopped on the way back to the kitchen to put the soap next to a full bottle of the same soap in the small laundry closet.

When I got back to the kitchen I found it empty. Following the sounds of voice I ended up in the living room. Trystan and Alison sat on the floor setting up a train set. Tyler sat across from them silently working on the same task. He regularly glanced up at Myra who was sitting on the sofa with her elbow propped on her knees.

I came up behind her and laid a hand on her shoulder. She stiffened for half a second before relaxing into the touch. 'Why does she still flinch? She should trust us by now.' Brooke said irritably.

'She does. It's instinctive, a learned response to physical contact. Don't take it so personally.' I responded calmly.

"Hey can I borrow you for a second?" I leaned down

whispering in Myra's ear.

I felt her shudder and heard her heart began racing. Her obvious reaction to me sent a thrill of excitement to every part of my body. I was glad that my sweats were baggy, overwise I would have been extremely uncomfortable.

She nodded to me before facing Tyler again.

"I'll be right back baby." She said with an encouraging smile.

Tryler nodded nervously.

"What's up?" Myra asked as we reached the hall.m

"Tyler asked me a question this morning and..." I paused unsure how to express my concerns. "I wasn't sure what you wanted to tell him."

I reached out twirling a strand of strawberry blonde hair around my finger.

"What about?" Her voice was hitched and I was suddenly aware that if Tyler wasn't in the next room waiting I would have my way with her all day.

Instead I step closer pushing her up against the wall and slip my fingers across her cheek.

"Us." My voice was lower than usual as I willed myself to take a step back.

It would have been simple enough to move away if she wanted that, but she made it clear she did not. She slid her fingers under my tank top trailing the waistband of my sweats. I groaned and closed my eyes, enjoying the sensation.

"Well," she whispered seductively into my ear. "That depends on what you want."

I sighed then grabbed her hand in mine and held it to my chest. "We need to talk about Ty."

She blushed, "I know, but the question remains. What do you want from this?"

I chuckled, "Not much, just a family and lifelong partnership."

She started to smile then stopped, "Are you sure. If we tell him that and you change you mind..."

She didn't have to finish. I could only imagine what that betrayal would do to the child's already frayed trust.

"What exactly did he ask?" She said before I could respond.

"If I was his new dad. I asked if that was what he wanted and he said yes." I relayed. Running my fingers across her cheek.

She smiled widely. "I never thought he would trust anyone as much as he does you."

"I think he knows that I already love him." I shrugged, embarrassed. "And I don't know how many times I have to tell you this before you believe me, but yes I'm serious. I'm not going anywhere."

Chapter 18

The Plan

We spent the day playing with Tyler, running the woods and all together getting to know each other better. I had never seen Myra so happy. I could feel the joy radiating off of her. She had everyone she cared about and trusted together under, and she was radiant.

That night, after Tyler was asleep, the four of us sat down around the kitchen table.

"We have to come up with a plan. If we just wing it no matter what, we lose to some degree." Alison said, all playfulness leaving her voice.

"What do you suggest?" I asked calmly.

"We have to leave Ty somewhere safe and draw Victor to us. The longer we wait the more time he has to try to find sympathetic wolves. Last we heard he was alone and had lost all credibility." Alison said with a wicked grin.

I shivered, *'Why is it that all the small statured women in my life could appear so terrifying.'*

'There women, they are always terrifying whether you can see it or not.' Brooke responded with a purr. He had been

inordinately content to remain quiet the last twenty-four hours. *'Why is Victor alone?'*

"Why do you say he's alone. We were of the belief that he had joined a group determined to enslave humans." I asked, glaring as Azreals face flashed through my mind.

'We'll deal with him after this is all over.' Brooke growled.

"He had, but his main goal had always been to find Myra and get her back. When he tried to convince them that she had to be a priority, he revealed how insane he was and they kicked him out. Azreal may want powerful allies, but not so badly he is willing to keep a liability around." Alison frowned clearly thinking about the bigger threat we would eventually have to face.

I looked around the table seeing everyone had similar expressions. With some effort Trystan grinned, "His own pack overthrew his leadership. He's lost everything."

"And is for that very reason still a threat. He has nothing left to lose and after years of…" Alison bit her lip searching for the right words, "Studying Myra, he knows all your weaknesses."

Myra shuddered next to me glaring down at the table. I could feel the vulnerability and shame flooding off of her.

My blood boiled in my ears and Brooke growled loudly. It wasn't until everyone looked at me that I realized it had been out loud. Trystan looked as if he returned the sediment, Alison looked sympathetic, and Myra seemed pleasantly surprised.

"So shouldn't Myra stay back with Tyler?" I asked, suddenly stressed.

"No," Alison said just as Myra was about to argue. "He knows her weaknesses and how to control her if she is captive. However, I assume you guys have been working on her control?"

I nodded.

"Then he won't know her strength, he'll never get close enough. The main concern is what he tells others, we have to deal with the problem before it grows." Alison concluded.

I didn't like how much sense she made. I wanted Myra as far away from all of this as possible.

'Idiot. Look at her. She needs this.' Brooke snapped as I thought this.

When I looked over I saw a fiery determination I had never seen burning deeply in Myra's eyes.

'What if she gets hurt?' I thought, desperate that at least my own wolf was on my side.

'Ask her that.' He challenged.

'She'd burn me to a crisp.' I rolled my eyes.

'My point exactly.' His satisfactory tone made me want to hit him before I decided it would hurt me more.

I sighed loudly.

"So are you on board?" Alison asked, stiffly.

I got the feeling she wasn't used to being doubted. Her annoyance amused me, but I bit back a sarcastic retort. This was a serious discussion and I would hate for any one of them to think I was taking it lightly. I had spent years trying to find my family, now it was time for me to defend it.

"So what's the plan." I relented leaning forward on the table.

Alison nodded and smirked, I had the feeling she had known what I almost said. It felt so weird talking to somebody who knew every direction the conversation could or could have gone.

""As I said first we need a place for Tyler." Alison replied.

"Rowan? I asked questioningly at Myra.

She nodded, "I can't take him there though can I?"

Alison looked uncomfortable as she shook her head. "Your scent is too familiar to him, if he crosses it he would follow it and…" She trailed off.

"I'll do it." I offered, "He doesn't know me at all."

"That is the best course." Alison nodded.

"God just tell us!" Myra snapped. "These guessing games are annoying."

Alison sighed, "Fine. Richard takes Tyler to his friend's place then meets us at cabin number three in his own pack's territory. We set the trap and wait."

"How do we contact him?" I asked.

"We know somebody who used to be in close standing with Victor and would do anything to get back in his good graces." Trystan surprised me by answering.

"You have contact with him?" Myra's voice was shocked and somewhat pained.

"I haven't contacted him but he asks after you regularly. I will give him what he wants. He won't even know he's setting up his own master's demise." Trystan said seriously.

Myra nodded and Alison laid her hand on his knee in a comforting gesture.

"Who?" I asked, feeling completely left out.

135

"The man who sold me to Victor in the first place." Myra said before looking up at me. "Our father

Laying out a Snare

The following day I got together Tylers stuff and held up as he bid farewell to Myra. At the point when he was clasped into the vehicle I went to her. She astonished me by bouncing into my arms.

I laughed, folding my arms over her midsection and pulling her nearer. I took in her fragrance and needed to remind myself I would be with her again around evening time.

"If it's not too much trouble, ensure he is protected. I'm believing you totally at this moment." She at last stifled out, tears thick in her voice.

"I will not allow anything to happen to him." I pulled away getting over a tear her cheek. "Guard yourself, I'll see you soon."

She gestured prior to inclining toward my hand.

"I love you." She murmured.

"I love you as well." I reacted then grinned attempting to comfort her. "This will work, it's Alison's arrangement, recall?"

She laughed, "No doubt, alright."

"I'll see you soon." With that I kissed her brow and moved into the vehicle.

The principal half hour of the drive was quiet as I permitted Tyler to attempt to deal with his sentiments.

"Are you amped up for your sleepover bud?" I at long last asked when the quiet appeared to be stunning.

He shrugged.

'Ask him what's up?' Brooke recommended after another long quietness.

"Are you alright Ty?" I asked all things considered.

He shrugged once more. This time I didn't push any farther. He plainly didn't have any desire to talk, and I wasn't one to compel it.

Time appeared to slither and I was amazed to take a gander at the clock and acknowledge just an hour had passed. Then, at that point, Tyler talked. His tormented voice interfered with my considerations and made my heart throb.

"Are you and my mom leaving me always?" His murmur was scarcely coherent.

"No Ty, we simply need to deal with something and we need you to be protected." I answered, amazed that in any event, knowing his frailties his words hurt. "We will be back in a few days tops. You will mess around with Avrily."

I realized it didn't make any difference what I said. It would require long stretches of demonstrating my words to make him positive about his own self-esteem. The outrage that underlying my chest, satisfied me that I would have the option to battle the one who caused Tylers question soon. At no other time had I held onto such a lot of disdain for someone I had never met.

Leaving Tyler with Rowan and Zane turned out more earnestly then I had anticipated. I was astonished to discover, as I maneuvered back onto the principle street, that I was crying. While I had never been told young men don't cry, it was an exceptionally uncommon thing for me.

Notwithstanding, heading out realizing he didn't really accept that I would be back killed me. I swiped at my eyes driving the feelings away until further notice. I had more significant issues close by then my sentiments.

***

At the point when I got to the house we had consented to meet at, I discovered Alison sitting on the patio scowling. At the point when I followed her look I saw Trystan and Myra contending by the timberline. Myra was talking stubbornly and pointed at him. In counter he smacked her hand away from her and throw his hand noticeable all around exasperated.

As I watched her recoil at his fast developments I battled the desire to step in.

"I wouldn't in case I were you. She'll simply get frantic that you'll agree with his stance." Alisons voice diverted me.

"What's going on with it?"

"She needs him to converse with her with regards to his inclinations toward their dad. He needs to shield her from subtleties in this manner will not open dependent upon her." She grinned looking depleted.

"That seems like his decision," I shrugged scowling at the kin. "In the event that he would not like to talk he doesn't need to."

"Clues why I said you should avoid it." She moaned laying her jawline on her knees.

"Is it accurate to say that you are OK?"

"Recently drained. Watching anybody all day, every day is debilitating, however attempting to watch the entire circumstance and change terrible endings is much harder." She shrugged.

I out of nowhere felt regretful. I hadn't understood how much exertion she was ousting for this intend to work.

"Is there anything we can do to facilitate the tension?" I
asked miserably.

She laughed pompously prior to looking at me. She read
me briefly then grinned brilliantly.

"What?" I asked, feeling like she was gazing directly
through me.

"I'm simply happy she discovered another provider."

I gestured uncertain how to react as I thought back up at
Myra who was all the while contending with her sibling.

"Do they do that alot?" I at last asked after one more
moment.

"They are kin." Alison shrugged.

I gestured prior to changing the subject. "So how did the contact go?"

"Great Trys had the option to tell his father the uplifting news." Her voice had another frosty tone.

"Uplifting news?" I didn't know I needed to know the appropriate response, however with the wild worry that consumed in Alison's eyes as she watched Trystan, I needed to know.

"That Trystan tracked down his tragically missing sister and she is entirely protected." Alison shrugged, reclining against the progression behind her. "Their dad professes to be stressed over her however reports back to Victor."

I gestured, attempting to overlook the annoyance holding my jaw.

Alison laughed, "Soon, don't do anything idiotic at this point."

"Like what?"

"On the off chance that you attempt to catch him, she will follow and she will see him first." Her voice was more earnest than I had anticipated.

"She could take him." I constrained a grin.

"No, he knows a lot about her shortcomings." Alison mumbled, gazing at the kin quarreling. "He read her for quite a long time. He knows precisely the stuff to strip her of every last bit of her force. I never at any point told Trystan this however Victor has mode Ember vanish for a month."

"That is incomprehensible." I wheezed, abruptly apprehensive for my mate.

"It's not. Both of you might be probably the most remarkable wolves out there, yet everybody has shortcomings. You are both more responsive to those shortcomings." She disclosed then went to take a gander at me.

"Consider the possibility that he educated others regarding these shortcomings of hers?" I sounded as terrified as I felt as Asriel's face streaked in my mind.

"He wouldn't." Alison grinned purposely, "His pride is his destruction. He won't ever surrender the fantasy about having a weapon no one but he can contain. He needs to utilize her against everybody. He could never surrender that force."

"How would you know? HJe might have as of now told…" I reacted feeling fairly less concerned.

She chuckled tapping her sanctuary, "I know him better than you can envision. The decisions individuals make uncover a great deal about them."

I gestured, and we sat peacefully for some time. In case I was following the contention right, Myra stressed over Trystan and he was irritated.

I giggled at its ludicrous ordinariness. Overprotective younger sibling and excessively irritated older sibling, I had seen it played out multiple times. Conceded the battles weren't ordinarily over the enthusiastic strength of a man conversing with his past victimizer.

I shivered at the idea. I had consistently been informed that the most grounded of individuals regularly had the hardest pasts. With that I investigated at Alison pondering abruptly what sort of life had formed the unphased, not set in stone lady sitting close to me. She concealed her dread so well I contemplated whether it was something she needed to do regularly.

"My ability was not permitted at my home. On the off chance that I predicted something, I got faulted for it. I figured out how to conceal my responses to my experiences." She shrugged. "I figured I would keep away from the brief respite while you discussed if to inquire. He'll be here soon. We need to stop them now."

She stood up skipping on her toes generous.

"Will I at any point become acclimated to that?" I asked logically.

"Two years and 90 days." She smiled generally, "Roughly."

I snickered then remained to join her as she strolled towards Myra and Trystan. Before we met them anyway she froze wide peered toward and turned abruptly.

"No," She said, looking befuddled and alarmed.

I turned towards the forest where a man with tan skin, thick dark twists, and radiant green eyes ventured out from between the trees. He was my tallness and would have been gorgeous notwithstanding the frenzied look that consumed in his eyes.

He strolled strongly into the clearing as though he had no dread on the planet, and I needed to let it out alarmed me. Myra squeaked frightened behind me.

Victor held a firearm up and I gazed stunned. Shots would just sting any of us, if that. Had he flipped out to the point he had failed to remember clear realities.

"NO!" Alison shouted.

As Victor pulled the trigger I recalled the thing she had said about him knowing Myra's shortcomings. Tungsten, I understood past the point of no return.

As the projectile struck Myra's arm however something much more crazy occurred. There was a little blast and the shot liquidized. Myra tumbled to the ground shaking as her lips became blue and her internal heat level noticeably dropped.

Quickly I constrained all of my energy on defrosting the ice precious stones that were currently leaking out of the injury in her arm. It took all of my energy to constrain the water to warm up.

Victor chuckled malignantly, "Cool right?"

"How did you deal with her?" I murmured through grasped teeth as Alison and Trystan raced to Myra's side.

"Goodness, simply a Tungsten slug with a little barium hydroxide octahydrate in the tip and ammonium thiocyanate in the base. Open effect the two touch and promptly transform into a freezing fluid. Much to cold for Ms. Ash here to stand." He smiled at me with those equivalent frenzied eyes. "Isn't science astonishing? I'm simply a straightforward researcher, the same as different werewolves. However I can contain both a maitre de fue and a maitre de l'eau."

150

Brooke snarled noisily through my teeth, however was too centered around keeping Myra alive to do substantially more.

"Go on. It would just pause for a minute to kill me." Victor insulted, "obviously then your taken prostitute may be dead."

He ventured forward so he was solidly in my face. "Attempt it."

Chapter 20

A Final Stand

"What do you say Richy? Are you going to draw out her hopeless life or discard the danger to her opportunity?" He murmured derangedly.

I swung at him, battling to not permit my focus on Myra to blur. I needed to save her, and I needed to overcome him.

"Gracious, we are noteworthy aren't we. No big surprise our dad needed you. However, mother realized you were unique as well. That is the reason she fled with you." His words curved in my gut like a blade.

"What?" I heaved.

"Goodness, father discovered her and she paid the consequences for her conspiracy. Notwithstanding, not before she figured out how to conceal you. I thought you were dead, sibling."

The word struck me like an actual blow and I tumbled to my knees. It must be completely false, however at that point for what reason did it bode well? Indeed, even to the reason behind Myra being drawn to him in any case. We shared blood so he would normally have a sense of security to my mate. Then, at that point, there was the way hard Myra had battled me, she had learned not to trust the sense of security around him, and me.

"No," I murmured regardless of realizing he was coming clean.

"That's right, father killed mother, I killed father. I'm the main family you have left."

With those words I saw Logan, Rowan, Myra, Tyler, and all of my pack to me. He wasn't right, I had a gigantic family and they were all able to follow me. Indeed, even Logan went with my impulses and never re-thought me.

With that, I felt a flood of recognizable energy however this time I didn't modest from it or push it away. I felt myself moving and becoming significantly bigger than Brooke had been. Abruptly the work I was placing into supporting Myra felt inadequate.

I remained in wolf structure eye to eye with the one who had manhandled and tortured the lady I cherished for quite a long time.

"Wha… " He heaved, venturing back so rapidly he fell on his butt.

Brooke growled boisterously.

"Father passed on years prior. I became alpha, not you!" His piercing yell showed his franticness.

He immediately recovered and moved. He was a hand more limited than me in any event.

'How are you an Alpha?' His wolf requested.

'I acquired your title when you destroyed father's pack, I additionally was allowed the title by my took on father.' Brooke snarled joyfully responding to the inquiry I wasn't ready to.

'That is impractical… ' Victor's voice rang with skepticism. 'No wolf can be the alpha without a pack! You gave your authority to that other person, and father's pack is history.'

'I will restart it. I will make it a place of refuge for any individual who needs it.' I countered. 'What's more, I have a pack.'

Similarly as I got done with talking Trystan, who had been sneaking up behind Victor, jumped on him. I jumped into the battle and for quite a while everything was lost abruptly of teeth, hooks, and blood.

When all that settled I ended up remaining over Victor's limp body. I looked at Trystan checking that he was OK, prior to strolling gradually to Myra.

Alison had figured out how to get the shot out of her arms and distant from her. I could in any case feel the virus transmitting off of her. I moved back rapidly tossing on my shorts.

"Is she going to be alright?" I asked quickly.

"Indeed, however Ember is gone." Her voice sounded broken and tormented.

"For how long?" I snapped.

"I don't have the foggiest idea… " She flinched, definitely realizing what might occur straightaway.

"How the fuck can you not know? Also, for what reason didn't you see this coming?!" I yelled holding up.

"I don't have a clue what occurred… " Her voice followed off. "He knew far beyond he ought to have. He discovered some way around me. He realized we were sitting tight for him."

"How?" I yelled at her, remaining over her as she sat on the ground close to Myra.

Some portion of me was happy when Trystan, presently in human structure, divided us pushing me back with two hands. A defensive growl tore through his teeth.

"Stop it, Richard. This isn't her shortcoming." He snapped. With overpowering agony and dissatisfaction, I felt destroys begin to run my cheeks.

"I can't lose her." My voice was stifled. "I can't."

"You will not." Trystan said certainly, "This isn't whenever Ember first has been gone, she will return. Myra will be fine."

With that I felt myself fold to my knees. I had never been more depleted in my life. I drug myself over to Myra's side and folded my arms over her.

I probably nodded off then since when I opened my eyes it was getting dull. Trysten and Alison were sitting a little ways away, talking discreetly.

"Richard?" Myra's voice was feeble, however regardless of that help washed over me.

"Myra?" I asked wildly.

Checking out I saw a huge cover hung over us and immediately pulled it up around her. She shuddered somewhat, cuddling into my chest.

"You should remain safe." I endeavored to berate her.

She laughed, "Me? Safe? I don't have a clue about the significance of the word."

I feigned exacerbation, yet couldn't resist the opportunity to grin. "You terrified me Myra."

"Sorry." She said genuinely.

I feigned exacerbation prior to kissing her profoundly. She froze shocked briefly prior to pulling me closer.

"So what do we do now?" She asked as I pulled away, meeting her warm earthy colored eyes once more.

"Presently we discover a shadow and fabricate our pack." I said unquestionably, "Victor is gone yet greater dangers are still out there, and we must be prepared for them."

She gestured apprehensively. I then again had never had an all the more sure outlook on anything in my life. However long I had Myra and Tyler, we could do anything.

THE END.